Mama's Chicken and Dumplings

Mama's Chicken and Dumplings

DIONNA L. MANN

MARGARET FERGUSON BOOKS
HOLIDAY HOUSE · NEW YORK

The publisher wishes to thank Dr. Scot French, Associate Professor, Department of History, University of Central Florida, for his expert help.

Margaret Ferguson Books

Copyright © 2024 by Dionna L. Mann
All Rights Reserved
HOLIDAY HOUSE is registered in the U.S. Patent and Trademark Office.
Printed and bound in June 2024 at Sheridan, Chelsea, MI, USA.
www.holidayhouse.com
First Edition
1 3 5 7 9 10 8 6 4 2

Library of Congress Cataloging-in-Publication Data

Names: Mann, Dionna L., author.
Title: Mama's chicken and dumplings / Dionna L. Mann.
Description: First edition. | New York : Margaret Ferguson Books/Holiday House, 2024. | Includes bibliographical references. | Audience: Ages 8–11. | Audience: Grades 4–6. | Summary: "Set in the 1930s in the African American community of Vinegar Hill in Charlottesville, Virginia, ten-year-old Allie devises a secret Man for Mama Plan to find her mama a husband"— Provided by publisher.
Identifiers: LCCN 2023023532 | ISBN 9780823455553 (hardcover)
Subjects: CYAC: Single-parent families—Fiction. | Mothers and daughters—Fiction. | African Americans—Fiction. | Charlottesville (Va.)—History—20th century—Fiction. | LCGFT: Historical fiction. | Novels.
Classification: LCC PZ7.1.M3659 Mam 2024 | DDC [Fic]—dc23
LC record available at https://lccn.loc.gov/2023023532

ISBN: 978-0-8234-5555-3 (hardcover)

In keeping with the historical record, the main character occasionally identifies people within her community as "colored" instead of African American or Black. The author, an African American herself, conscientiously strove to use the term sparingly, only when it seemed absolutely necessary to the story, and never with the intent to make young readers feel ill at ease.

The photo on pg. 188 is used with permission of the estate of George C. Seward, found in the George C. Seward Photograph Collection, Albert and Shirley Small Special Collections Library, University of Virginia.

♥

To David C., my same-age cousin, who all while I was growing up was my solace, my laughter, and my friend, especially when things in my life felt broken.

Mama's Chicken and Dumplings

one
Pinching Pennies

I'm sitting on our front stoop, brushing my doll Mitzy's hair, when Mr. Gray, the rent man, comes, smiling his fat smile. He *floomp-paloomps* his great big body up the steps. Who does he think he is, almost squishing my fingers?

"You're excused," I say, though he didn't ask to be.

When Mr. Gray knocks, Mama doesn't answer. That's because she's hanging up clothes on the clothesline out back. But I've decided I'm not getting Mama. I'm ignoring Mr. Gray just like he's ignoring me.

Besides, Mr. Gray doesn't deserve one red cent of my mama's hard-earned money. He never fixes anything around here. But you watch. Mama will soon be handing Mr. Gray every bit of our rent money just like she always does.

I hate the way my mama has to pinch pennies just to pay the rent on this run-down excuse for a house.

Do you think Mr. Gray cares that my daddy ran off like a no-good nobody when I was five years old, then got himself killed, leaving my mama to scrub and wash and sew and clean, working her fingers to the bone all by herself?

No.

Do you think Mr. Gray cares that I never have two cents to buy a couple of Mary Janes from the jars of penny candy lined up inside Mr. Inge's grocery store?

No.

Do you think he cares that I don't have my own flute, and can't practice for the school band all summer?

No.

Do you think he cares about my mama and me?

No.

All he cares about is collecting his rent.

Too bad Mama can't afford her own house here in Charlottesville like some of the other colored folks in my neighborhood, like Gwen Turner, my NOT-friend. She lives in a nice brick house on Commerce Street, all because her daddy's a builder. I'm sure Gwen's daddy can fix anything that gets broken down at her house.

Her daddy has so much money, Gwen gets to buy bags full of candy whenever she wants. She wears different-colored store-bought dresses with matching ribbons every day at school. She even has her own flute. Why can't I have a daddy like Gwen's?

I've seen Mr. Turner walking through town with his wife and four daughters. I've seen him kind-smiling at them, paying attention whenever one of them is talking, holding them if they're crying. I've even seen him break out with a silly song when he wants to make one of his daughters laugh. On top of having a daddy like that, Gwen's uncle Mr. Coles, our band teacher, treats her like a daughter, too! It's like Gwen has two daddies. And me? I don't have one!

Just thinking on it makes my inside heat rise.

Mr. Gray knocks again. I start to hum a song to take the lid off my thoughts. They're bubbling inside me like black-eyed peas simmering in a pot.

Just as my inside heat starts cooling, Mr. Gray clears his throat and says, "Run along, missy. Fetch your mother for me."

And just like that I'm hot again.

It's the way Mr. Gray says *missy* like he thinks he's better than Mama and me. *Run along, missy. Fetch your mother for me.* Ha! I'm not running anywhere for you, Mr. Gray.

Mr. Gray stares at me. "Late rent comes with a fee," he says.

"Mama's out back," I say, giving in. "I'll go get her, but I'm not running, I'm skipping."

Mr. Gray laughs, though I wasn't meaning it to be funny.

I hop down the steps, and skip around the side of the house toward Mama. While I'm skipping, I'm thinking on Mr. Johnson at Odin Johnson's Antiques. He opened his store down on West Main Street this summer and he's nothing like Mr. Gray.

First of all, Mr. Johnson never stinks of men's cologne. Second, Mr. Johnson is a fixer. He fixes big things like dressers with broken legs. Medium things like lamps with broken wires. And small things like dolls with missing eyelashes. My best friend Jewel and I have watched him do it. We like to go into his store and make up stories about the old-timey things he sells. Third, every time Jewel and I visit, we catch him happy-singing, unless he's with a customer. And the fourth and most important thing is that Mr. Johnson never ignores me. How I wish Mama would marry someone like Mr. Johnson. Then I'd never have to worry about pennies being pinched or being stuck in a broken-down house. My days would be brimmed with happy.

"Mama," I say after I get around back, "Mr. Gray is here."

"Gracious me!" Mama says. "Time got away from me."

She drops my wet Sunday dress into the clothes basket and places her clothespins back into her apron pocket. She smooths herself out, pats her hair down, and walks toward Mr. Gray.

"I don't like Mr. Gray," I say to Mama, following her.

"Hush your mouth, child," Mama says, though I'm pretty sure, deep-down, she feels the same way.

After Mama hands Mr. Gray the rent money, he joggles toward the next run-down house he owns. When he reaches the sidewalk where some girls are singing "On the Good Ship Lollipop," and some boys are playing marbles, he does what he always does. He sticks his fat hand into his pocket and pulls out a handful of pennies. He throws them into the air, and the boys and girls—all with skin in shades of brown, like mine—scatter. I can hear Mr. Gray laughing, even though he's halfway down my block, Third Street NW. Would he, I wonder, throw those pennies if those kids had the same color skin as he did?

Mama, still behind me, makes a three-steps-down sound on her I'm-not-approving-of-this ladder. "*Uhn-uhn-uhn*, like little mice after cheese." Then she points her finger at me. "I better never catch you picking up Mr. Gray's pennies. You hear me?"

"Yes, ma'am," I say, though I'm thinking mice are happy when they find cheese, unless there's a trap.

two
PRACTICALLY PERFECT

On Sundays, Mama and I always cook together after church. If Uncle John is picking us up to go to his and Aunt Lavern's house in the country for Sunday supper, I might help Mama make homemade rolls or an apple cobbler or a sweet potato pie to take over.

In the summer, I especially love going there. That's because I don't get to see my cousin Caesar like I do when we're in school. Caesar is more like my twin brother than my cousin. He's ten, just like me, and we even have the same oval birthmark—mine is on my right arm, his is on his left. His real name is Julius Caesar, but never mind his fancy name. He's no emperor. He's just plain old Caesar to me.

But even better than Sundays at Caesar's are Sundays like today when it's just Mama and me and we're making chicken and dumplings for supper. These kinds of Sundays are practically perfect. I say "practically" because there's an important piece missing.

"Mama?" I ask, while buttoning up Mitzy's just-ironed dress. "Wouldn't it be perfect if you got married? Then you wouldn't have to work every day, morning until night, Monday through Friday. Your husband would have enough money to buy you nice things. I could have my own flute. We'd be living in a fine house—nothing broken-down inside it. Best of all, there'd be no empty spot at the kitchen table. Wouldn't that be perfect?"

Mama washes her hands, still sticky with grease from pulling chicken off the bones. She nods toward the place at our kitchen table where there's a third chair.

"You call that an empty spot? That's what I call extra room for Mitzy."

"Don't be silly, Mama," I say. "Mitzy doesn't need a spot. She's not real."

Of course, it wasn't that long ago that I used to think Mitzy could hear me whenever I was pouring out my heart to her, but now that I'm ten, I know better.

"But what if," I say, "what if you had a husband like Aunt Lavern has Uncle John, like Gwen's mama, Mrs. Turner, has Mr. Turner? You need someone like that, Mama."

Mama walks away from the kitchen counter, leans over, and kisses my forehead. "No, Alexandra Lewis, I do not."

"But if you found a *perfect* man to marry...he'd come into the house at night after working all day. He'd have a kind smile when he saw you cooking for him. He'd love our chicken-and-dumpling Sundays. Best of all, he'd sing silly songs to make you laugh whenever you were sad."

"Your imagination has gotten away from you!" Mama says. "There's no such thing as perfect. Now put Mitzy away and get started on the dumplings."

"Yes, ma'am," I say, though I'm pretty sure Mama is wrong. There is perfect out there, and it's waiting for Mama and me. I know it is, because I can feel it *tapa-tapa*-tapping inside my chest.

I put Mitzy in a chair, wash my hands, and take out the ingredients to get started on the dumplings. I don't take out the little stool to stand at the counter because nowadays I'm tall enough without it. I also don't take out a recipe. That's because I know just how much flour and shortening and cooled-down chicken broth to use—no need for measuring cups.

When I'm finished putting the ingredients into the bowl, I use my fingers to make a crumbly mixture. I sprinkle some flour on the counter, then turn the mixture out, and work it into a smooth ball of dough.

I get out the rolling pin that Grandpa made for Grandmama as a gift for their wedding day. (I can't believe she didn't bonk him on the head with it! A rolling pin for a wedding present. Whoever heard of such a thing? But I do like to hear Mama tell the story.)

I feel the handles push the pin over the dough as I'm rolling out a perfect-dumpling thickness. I begin to wonder, as I often do when Mama and I make chicken and dumplings, what was my grandpa like? He certainly wasn't very romantic. But was he a kind man? Did he like to sing? Did he love my grandmama's chicken and dumplings? Did he like to watch my mama when she was a little girl and was rolling out dumpling dough like I'm rolling now?

Sometimes while I'm practicing my flute during the school year, I like to imagine my grandparents sitting in front of me: eyes closed, heads nodding, bodies swaying like they're listening to church music. I wish I could see my grandpa's face when I'm imagining, but he was gone and buried before I was born. I remember Grandmama though—the way her eyes turned into little slits when she smiled, the way her brown wrinkly skin draped over her knobby knuckles, the way she could comb her hair through without using any heat. She died when I was six, before I started playing the flute.

Grandmama was always saying, had Grandpa been alive when my daddy took off, he would've chased that rascal down and made him keep his promise to take care of Mama and me. For some reason, whenever Grandmama said "rascal," it made me laugh, even though being lousy at taking care of your family is no laughing matter.

What if Grandpa hadn't died when he did? Would my life be better now? I sigh a long sigh. Thinking on the what-ifs always makes me want to cry.

Once I've got the dumpling dough rolled out, I take a butter knife and begin to slice it into rectangles. First I make long cuts from top to bottom, then from side to side. I'm trying my best to make each dumpling the same size. Mama looks over at me while I work.

"Will you stop worrying yourself with perfection?" she says. "They look fine!"

"Dumplings need to be perfect, Mama," I say. "They taste better that way."

Mama shakes her head and laughs a little. "Go ahead and start dropping them in," she says. "The broth is boiling."

With each dumpling *palop-palop*-plopping into the pot, I get a whiff of Mama's delicious cooking. *Mmm, mmm!* While

I'm dropping in dumplings, Mama is adding the chicken. Though we're working over the same pot, it's perfectly fine. We know how to work like that, bumping elbows and being in each other's way.

When I'm done, I sit down at the table, put Mitzy on my lap, and watch Mama stir the dumplings so they won't stick to each another. As I do, an idea starts brewing inside me. It's an answer to all my what-ifs and wishes—a Man-for-Mama Plan as warm as bread dough proving beneath a dish towel. And it's going to turn out perfect. I'm sure because I can feel it rising!

three
OBVIOUSLY

It's Monday morning, and like she always does during the week, Mama has gone over to work at Mrs. McIntire's house. And, as usual, Miss Greta from next door has come over to keep an eye on me, though her eyes will close as soon as she gets comfortable in the chair that used to be Grandmama's. I was glad when Aunt Lavern gave Mama that chair after Grandmama passed. Whenever I sit in it, I feel like a small piece of Grandmama is still wrapped around me.

After Miss Greta and I have some oatmeal, I head to my best friend Jewel's house on Williams Street. My Man-for-Mama Plan is safe inside my dress pocket. I wrote it up last night after Mama kissed me good night, and now it's itching to get out. I can't wait to tell Jewel all about it! But I'm not spilling the beans until we're sitting in our favorite spot just beyond the swings and beneath the big old oak tree—our tree—at Washington Park. It's the perfect place for sharing secrets with Jewel.

I bet that oak tree has heard a hundred years' worth of secrets, ever since it first started growing back in the 1830s. Its trunk is wide enough for both Jewel and me to sit side by side, lean our backs on it, and get comfortable. When we do, we like to imagine, or share our deep-down thoughts, like what scares us, or what makes us mad, or what we wish for.

It was under that tree that Jewel told me she hates snakes, even black ones that eat mice, and how she worries they're creepy-crawling under her bed at night. She's told me how mad she gets when squirrels jump into her grandfather's strawberry patch and eat all the juicy sweet fruit no sooner than it's red. She's told me how she wishes she could remember her parents and her grandmother, who all died from the flu when she was just a baby.

Of course, I tell Jewel my secrets, too—how I wish I'd never been born to a no-good daddy. How I wish my mama would marry a good man. How I wish for my own flute. She can't understand why I'm not happy with just Mama and me and I have never been able to explain it in a way that makes sense to her.

I know it's foolish to wish for things that can't be changed, like wishing that my grandparents were alive, or that Mama had married a good man. But wishing for things I can change and working to make them come true... well, that's another matter altogether.

When I get to Jewel's house, I loud-knock.

Like always, her grandfather Mr. Poindexter hollers through the door. "Come in!"

"It's me, Mr. Poindexter... Allie," I say as I open the door.

No sooner do I get inside, than here comes Jewel with half of her hair braided, barreling down the stairs to greet me.

"Hey!" she says. "Come on up!"

And I do.

I sit on her bed and start bouncing while she finishes her hair.

"I've got something to show you!" I say between bounces.

"What is it?" she asks, looking at my reflection in her mirror.

"I can't tell you. Your grandfather might hear."

"He can't hear you! He can hardly hear at all. Is it *top secret*?"

"Top."

"Can you give me clue?" She catches the end of her braid with a hair tie.

I try to think of a clue.

"*Hmm*. One plus one makes two. Two plus one makes three, and three is me."

"What kind of clue is that?"

"Why'd you ask for a clue if you're not even going to try to guess?"

"*Three is me*. That's no clue. That's a riddle."

"Riddle. Clue. All the same," I say. "Will you hurry up so we can go to the park. I'll tell you about it once we get there."

When she's done with her hair, Jewel puts on her shoes and buckles them. Then we hop downstairs to ask Mr. Poindexter for permission to go to the park. Though it's still morning time, he's already at the kitchen sink, cleaning greens from his garden.

Jewel says, "Gramps, Allie and I are headed to the park. Is that okay with you?"

Instead of answering, Mr. Poindexter grumbles about needing some fatback.

"Gramps," Jewel says again, louder this time. "Can I go to the park with Allie?"

"Go on, child, but don't stay all day. I'll need your help in the garden this afternoon."

"Yes, sir," Jewel and I say, and we're out the door.

Under a bright blue sky, we run down Williams Street. We run up Fourth Street. We skip all the way down Preston Avenue until we're finally at Washington Park. We walk to our tree, plop down, and wait for our huffing and puffing to slow.

Jewel—sitting beside me, shoulder to shoulder—wipes her sweaty forehead and says, "Well? What's your secret?"

I pull part one of my Man-for-Mama Plan out from my dress pocket. It's a map of Vinegar Hill and all the shops owned by colored folks on our stretch of West Main Street.

Jewel quick-takes it from me, unfolds it, and looks it over. "What's this?" she says. Then she reads what's at the top of the paper. "Man-for-Mama Plan—Part One." Jewel looks at me like I've done lost my mind. "Seriously? Whose mama are you talking about?"

"Mine, obviously."

Jewel turns my plan sideways. "How's a map of our neighborhood going to help you find your mama a husband?"

"It's like a treasure map. Don't you see the red heart I drew right above Odin Johnson's Antiques? The heart is like an *X* marking the spot."

"Oh, I see the heart now," Jewel says. "Still, I don't get it. How's a heart on a map going to help your mama get married? I mean, Mr. Johnson is nice and all, but…"

"But what? It's a perfect plan. You'll see."

I reach into my dress pocket, pull part two of my plan out, and start reading it to her.

"Step one: Jewel and Allie will interview gentlemen who work on West Main Street so we can find four more gentlemen suitable for Mama. Step two: Allie will add a red heart above each suitable man's place of business and a black heart over the businesses where the gentlemen aren't suitable. The reason I want four more prospects," I explain to Jewel, "even though I've already drawn a red heart for Mr. Johnson, is because I think we should find five possible suitors in all. Four plus one being five."

"Of course four plus one is five!" Jewel's head shakes a little when she says it.

"Just clarifying," I say. "Step three: Jewel and Allie will bake sugar cookies at Jewel's house."

She butts in. "Why are we baking at my house?"

"I have to keep this a secret from my mama, and I don't want Miss Greta getting wind of it. Can I finish now?"

Jewel says, "You can finish."

"Step four: Jewel and Allie will sell the sugar cookies."

Jewel butts in again. "And where do you suppose we'll sell them?"

"On your lawn, obviously, like a lemonade stand."

"Okay. Continue."

"Step five: Jewel and Allie will use the money they get from selling the cookies to buy the ingredients to make chicken and dumplings.

"Step six: Jewel and Allie will make chicken and dumplings at Jewel's house.

"Step seven: Jewel and Allie will deliver a jar of chicken and dumplings to each potential man for Mama.

"Step eight: Jewel and Allie will discuss the suitable gentlemen and narrow the list down to one.

"Step nine: Jewel and Allie will introduce Mama to THE ONE. (Probably Mr. Johnson.)

"Step ten: Jewel and Allie will help Mama plan her wedding."

I look over at Jewel. "What do you think? Sound like a good plan to you?"

Jewel blinks a few times likes she trying to decide if it's a good plan or not. "I think it's too many steps."

"It's not."

"And how do you suppose we're going to find gentlemen suitable for your mama? That's not logical at all! We're only ten years old!"

"I've already figured that part out," I say. "Let me read what I wrote at the bottom here: While talking with the gentlemen on West Main Street, Jewel and Allie will check to see if they have a kind smile. They will find out if they like to sing. They will make sure they can fix things."

"And why are we delivering chicken and dumplings to these potential suitors? What does that have to do with anything?"

"You should know the answer to that one! Any man good enough for my mama must love her chicken and dumplings."

"What if they all love the chicken and dumplings? How does that help us narrow the list down to one? It doesn't make any sense!"

I squint my eyes at Jewel. "Why are you being so negative?"

"I'm not being negative, just logical! You asked me what I thought, didn't you?"

"I thought it all out, and it's a perfect plan."

"How are we going to know whether or not they have a wife at home? Have you thought about that? There aren't too many single men your mama's age. I mean, your mama's no spring chicken."

"She's no old maid either! She's only twenty-nine!" I say. "As to knowing if he's got a wife at home..." I hold up my left hand and point to my ring finger. "Make sure he's not wearing a wedding ring right here, that's how!"

"Right...," Jewel says.

"Well? What do you think? Are you in?"

Jewel scratches her head like she's still not sure, but then her face bursts out with a smile. "For you, I'm in! When do we start?"

"Tomorrow," I say.

four
MAN-FOR-MAMA PLAN

The next morning, I tell Miss Greta goodbye and go to Jewel's house, where I wait outside while she's finishing her hair. I sit on her porch and peek inside my bag to make sure I've got everything we'll need to find four more eligible bachelors.

Do I have two cheese sandwiches, one for Jewel and one for me?

Check.

Do I have my map?

Check.

Do I have a red crayon for drawing red hearts over the businesses where the gentlemen who might be a good fit work?

Check.

Do I have a black crayon for drawing black hearts over the businesses where the gentlemen aren't right for Mama?

Check.

Do I have a photograph of Mama?

Check.

Most importantly, do I have Mitzy, looking fine in her clean but faded blue dress and braided hair? Of course. Even if Mama says I'm too old for her, I would never forget Mitzy. Not on a day like today.

Just as I'm done checking my bag, Jewel comes outside. "Ready to add hearts to your daddy map?" she asks.

"Daddy map? Who said it was a daddy map? I'm not looking for a daddy. It's my Man-for-Mama Plan."

"Same thing," she says.

"No it's not."

"Yes it is."

"No it's not!"

"Think about it," she says. "If your mama gets married, won't you be getting a daddy?"

I put a hand on my hip. "It's a Man-for-Mama Plan, NOT a daddy map. Period."

"Same thing," Jewel says again.

"If my mama gets married, who says I'm calling him Daddy. I might call him Pa."

"You might call him Daddy. You're always talking about how you want to replace your no-good daddy with a good daddy."

"Never mind! We've got a lot to do! Let's go!"

While we're walking toward West Main Street, I notice the sky. It's as bright a blue as Mitzy's dress once was, and there're white fluffy clouds with no hint of rain. I notice the breeze. It's smelling sweet of peaches ready for picking. It's as if the not-too-hot sun is smiling down on Jewel and me. It's as if the August day knows. Rain or sticky heat won't do on the day I'm starting my Man-for-Mama Plan.

"I packed us cheese sandwiches," I say when we're halfway there.

"You think of everything!" Jewel says. "What else did you bring in that poor excuse for a bag?"

"Poor excuse? It's a perfectly good toting bag. Not a hole anywhere."

"Too bad it's not a patent-leather pocketbook like the one Dr. Stratton's wife carries on Sundays, the kind that matches your shoes and goes with a fancy hat." Jewel starts pretend-walking like she's Dr. Stratton's wife strolling with her husband.

Jewel in her I'm-a-lady voice says to a man in bib overalls who's walking toward us, "Good day, sir. Lovely weather, isn't it?"

"Indeed, it is!" he says, then tips his hat as if Jewel really is grown.

Jewel and I burst out laughing.

"What was that about?" I ask her.

"Just practicing," she says. "For when I'm older."

"After my mama gets married," I say, "I bet she'll carry a patent-leather handbag and wear a store-bought hat."

"Maybe when you get older you will," Jewel says. "I hope to carry a handbag and a doctor's bag."

"I believe you will," I say.

Pretty soon, Jewel and I near the part of West Main Street where all the buildings stand together like musicians in a marching band. There's a shop that sells and cleans beautiful hats. There's a tailor's shop that can take a man's suit that's three sizes too big and turn it into a perfect fit. There's an eating house that sells éclairs and tiny cakes and cucumber sandwiches. There's a shop that can fix the soles of your shoes and another one for shining them. There's a furniture store for setting up house, a barbershop and a beauty parlor to make you look your finest, and, of course, Mr. Inge's grocery store that sells the best produce and meats in all of Charlottesville. All put together, the different brick and wood buildings on West Main Street play an upbeat song that makes me want to sing.

I love West Main Street. It goes clean down to Preston Avenue and ends where East Main Street begins. West Main Street is the opposite of East Main Street or Market Street in downtown Charlottesville. Here we can go inside any shop we want to and nobody will follow us around like we're about to steal something. No one will say we can't sit down and share a milkshake. No one will say, *Get out, your kind aren't welcome here.* None of that on West Main. Even when white folks come to shop here no one says a thing. Everybody's welcome here.

"Oh!" Jewel says, "I forgot to tell you. My grandfather gave me four pennies for candy—two for me and two for you!"

"Mr. Poindexter is all right!" I say, and my mouth begins to water as I imagine us buying Mary Janes later.

Once we are near Gilt Edge Barbershop, we stop walking. I take out my map.

"Okay," I say. "I think we should try Journey's Used Sewing Machine Shop and Repairs first." I point to it on my map. "Mr. Journey must know how to fix things."

Jewel's face turns to looking worried. "Are you absolutely sure about this plan?"

"Absolutely sure," I say. "My mama deserves a good life."

I reach into my bag and take out my mama's eighth-grade graduation photograph and show it to Jewel. Mama looks beautiful with her hair done up fine, standing there in a lovely, long white dress, and holding her Jefferson School diploma. No one looking at the photograph, taken at Holsinger Studio, would know the dress with its white lacy collar was a hand-me-down, except maybe my aunt Lavern, who had worn it when she graduated before Mama did. Too bad my grandparents didn't know anyone in the North their daughters could live with so they could attend high school there. Mama always said had there been a Jefferson School that went past eighth grade back then, she probably wouldn't have married so young, probably would've become a teacher or an accountant. But then, she said, she wouldn't have been blessed with me. Mama never worries about the what-ifs in life.

Jewel takes the photograph. "Your mom used to be pretty," Jewel says.

"*Used to be?* She's still pretty."

"I didn't say she wasn't," Jewel says.

"Yes, you did! You said she 'used to be.'"

"Well, she used to be *real* pretty," Jewel says. "Anyway, why did you bring it? It might get ruined in that ugly bag."

"How's it going to get ruined in a frame? And my bag is not ugly!" I say.

"Yes it is."

"No it's not." Then I go on to explain why I brought the photograph in my not-ugly bag. "I want to show it to the gentlemen we think worthy of a red heart. That way they can see what a catch they'll be getting if they marry Mama!"

"That's a good idea," Jewel says.

I put Mama's picture away. "Here's what you'll do. If I give you a sign like this"—I bring my hands together and make a little heart with my fingers and thumbs—"that means the man we're talking to will get a red heart on my map. That's when you should reach into my bag, pull out my mama's photograph, then show it to him—casual-like."

"What? You want *me* to be the one to show them your mama's picture? Shouldn't you do it?"

"If you do it, we'll be working together."

Jewel thinks on it. "Okay. I'll do it."

And we walk toward Journey's.

five
JOURNEY'S USED SEWING MACHINE SHOP AND REPAIRS

I push open the heavy door.

"Hello there," a thin man dusting sewing machines says as soon as we walk in.

Right away, I peek at his left hand to see if he's wearing a wedding ring. He's not.

"What can I do for you young ladies?" he asks.

Jewel replies, "Oh, we're just browsing...," then whispers to me, "...for a bachelor."

I squint my eyes and *shoosh* her for being so forward.

But she just keeps on whispering. "Go on, see what he's like." Then she walks away toward the sewing machines for sale.

And so here I am, left by myself, eyes looking up at a man who's looking down at me.

"Do you sew?" he asks me.

"Oh...a little, but—I—" My heart is galloping.

Thankfully, Jewel comes and stands beside me, which makes my plan feel back on track.

"Her mother sews beautifully," Jewel says. "Have you

heard of Mrs. McIntire who lives on Rugby Road in that great big house?"

Mr. Journey says, "Is she the wife of Paul McIntire who donated the land for our park?"

"Yes, that's her," Jewel says.

"I've heard of her."

"Allie's mama makes her beautiful dresses."

"Is that right?" he says, still dusting.

"Yes, sir," I say, picking up where Jewel left off. "My mama cleans and cooks for her, too. Mrs. McIntire says my mama makes the world's best chicken and dumplings."

"That's nice," Mr. Journey says, and he kind-smiles.

Check.

"I'm wondering, Mr. Journey," I say. "I mean, it's obvious you know a thing or two about fixing things…but can you sing?"

Mr. Journey stops dusting and looks at Jewel and me like we're a math equation he's trying to figure. "Every now and again, I sing with Sampson's Happy Pals."

"I play the flute," I say. "And Jewel plays the sax."

"Music is food for the soul," he says.

I'm liking this Mr. Journey. So I turn to Jewel, who's now standing near spools of threads lined up in rows on Mr. Journey's wall. I give her the sign. Jewel hesitates, then comes over, sticks her hand in my bag, and grabs Mama's photograph.

"This is what Allie's mama used to look like," Jewel says. "Just in case you're wondering."

Mr. Journey takes Mama's picture. "You have a beautiful mother," he says. He hands it back while raising one eyebrow, which makes me wonder if he's figured out my plan. "Tell her if she needs a new machine or a repair to come on by and see Mr. Francis Journey."

"I will," I say. "But maybe you'd like to try the chicken and dumplings we were talking about. Jewel and I can bring you a jar. You sure could use some fattening up."

I feel Jewel's elbow in my ribs.

"Oh, sorry about that," I say. "But it's true, Mr. Journey. You're awfully thin."

Mr. Journey gives us a smile that's more zigzagged than curved, then says, "If you girls want to drop some home cooking off, I'd be happy to give it a try."

"I'm pretty sure you'll love it," I say. "Bye, Mr. Journey. It's been a real pleasure meeting you."

"Likewise," Mr. Journey says. "Your visit's been most interesting."

Once we're out of Mr. Journey's shop, Jewel and I sit down on the curb. I take out my map and red crayon, and add heart number two to my map. Only three more to go!

"So where to next?" Jewel asks after I'm done coloring the heart in. "Want to go to Frye's Meat Market?"

"You know full well that Josephine Frye's daddy has a wife and ten kids!"

"But Mr. Scott with his ice truck might be there. I don't think he's married."

"Mr. Scott is way too grumpy to be anybody's husband."

"But think of all the ice cream you could make if your daddy delivered ice!"

"I'm not looking for a daddy, remember," I say. "I'm looking for a husband for my mama."

Jewel and I take a few minutes to study my map and decide Mr. Brown's Shoe Repair is next.

"Let's eat our sandwiches before we go embarrassing ourselves again," Jewel says. "I'm starving!"

"We aren't embarrassing ourselves. What makes you think that?"

"Just the way it felt to hand Mr. Journey that photograph," she says.

"You did great!" I say. "I didn't feel the least bit embarrassed. And you know why?"

"Why?"

"Because Jewel Poindexter, my very best friend, is right beside me, helping me with my plan."

"You're a mess, Allie Lewis. A complete mess."

To get to the sandwiches, I take Mitzy out of my bag. Instead of putting her back, I squeeze her between Jewel and me. I hand Jewel her sandwich, then take out mine. We unwrap the brown paper from them and begin munching.

When I'm about a quarter of the way through my sandwich, a streetcar grumbles past, filling my ears with a brass-band sound, loud and clangy, but nice at the same time. When I'm about halfway through, a farmer driving an oxcart filled with watermelons *calump-calump-calumps* past. Right as our sandwiches are done, a shiny black automobile comes rolling toward us. In the passenger seat, a white boy sees us sitting on the curb and waves. We wave back. As soon as we do, his father slaps the back of his head.

"I hope he doesn't get in trouble just for being friendly," I say.

"He already did," Jewel says. Then she hands me her empty wrapper. "Let's go get our candy now!"

"Not yet! We only have two red hearts on the map, so we have a lot more stores to visit after Mr. Brown's. And we've got to go by Mr. Johnson's, too, so you can show him my mama's photograph. Mary Janes have to wait."

"Let's get started, then," Jewel says after sighing, and we head toward Mr. Brown's shoe shop.

six
Bells Ringing

By late afternoon, Jewel and I have checked out the gentlemen working inside ten more stores. We've added seven black hearts to my map for unsuitable gentlemen and three more red hearts for potential ones, bringing my red-heart total up to five—just like I'd planned.

"Can we get our Mary Janes now?" Jewel asks. "This matchmaking business is beating my feet up!"

I stop and face Jewel. "Have we shown Mr. Johnson my mama's photograph yet? No, we have not!"

"Seriously, Allie. I can't take much more of this."

"If you hadn't worn your Sunday shoes," I say, "your feet wouldn't be hurting!"

Jewel squints her eyes at me, so I soften my voice. "We won't stay long, promise."

"Fine. But you owe me one of your Mary Janes."

"Deal," I say.

When we walk into Odin Johnson's Antiques a bell above the door rings. Mr. Johnson is sitting at his worktable with a bright lamp shining down on it. Before him are tiny tools and tiny jars of paint. He's painting a small metal horse, making it look new. He looks up at us, takes his glasses off, and wide-smiles.

"Hello, Miss Allie, Miss Jewel." His words are almost singing.

"Good afternoon, Mr. Johnson!" I say a little louder than I was expecting.

He stands up and places his glasses on the counter next to his cash register. "How can I help you lovely ladies this afternoon? Mitzy need fixing?"

Last time Jewel and I were here, Mitzy's arm had popped out. Mr. Johnson fixed her without even charging me. That's the kind of man Mr. Johnson is. I take Mitzy out of my bag, and place her on the table, so Mr. Johnson can see that I've been taking good care of her.

"She's fine," I say. "Thanks for asking."

Jewel, obviously in a hurry to get to Mr. Inge's grocery store, interrupts saying, "Allie's got something to show you."

I squint my eyes at Jewel because I didn't give her the signal and she's the one who is supposed to show the photograph to Mr. Johnson.

"Oh?" Mr. Johnson's eyebrows squinch a little. "What is it?"

"Go on. Show him," Jewel says to me while leaning on his counter.

I shake my head because this is Jewel's part of the plan.

Jewel huffs, stuffs her hand into my bag, pulls out Mama's picture, and slaps it on the counter in front of Mr. Johnson. "Allie wants you to see what her mama looks like," she says.

And then, just then, something wonderful happens, something as beautiful as butterfly wings, something as sweet as pastries stuffed with cream, something as unexpected as snow in spring.

Mr. Johnson is saying, "Goodness me! This is your mother, Allie? I know this beautiful woman!"

"You do?" I say, surprised since Mr. Johnson just opened his shop this summer.

He says, "Oh, yes! We went to school together. How I loved teasing her! She couldn't stand it."

My words fly out. "Mr. Johnson! You know my mama? Really?"

"Sure do. She used to kick me in the shins when I made her mad." Mr. Johnson leans over the counter and whispers like he is telling us a secret. "I thought she was the prettiest girl in Virginia. I've been away from Charlottesville for so long after graduating from Jefferson School, I lost track of my old schoolmates. Who did little Lizzie end up marrying?"

And without warning, my inside heat rises, and I'm blurting out: "A no-good nobody who ran off when I was little, then got himself killed—that's who!"

"Oh, I'm sorry," Mr. Johnson says, all serious. Then he puts his glasses back on like he's about to start working again.

Jewel pipes up. "What Allie means to say, Mr. Johnson, is that her mama is *si-ing-gle*! And Allie wants to find her a husband who can fix things. Actually, you're Allie's first pick!"

Mr. Johnson laughs then. "I don't know what to say."

"Me either," I say, looking hard at Jewel for being so forward.

"It would be nice," Mr. Johnson says, "to see Lizzie again. But I must confess, I may be what folks call a confirmed bachelor."

"A what?" Jewel asks.

"A confirmed bachelor—a man that never marries."

"Well, that would be a shame," Jewel says.

"Don't say that, Mr. Johnson," I say, agreeing with Jewel.

"You just haven't found the right woman yet."

"Who knows," Jewel says, "maybe Allie's mama is the one!"

Mr. Johnson laughs again. "Well, tell your mother that Odin Johnson, from way back, has returned to Charlottesville, and says hello."

"I will!" Jewel and I say at the exact same time, which makes Mr. Johnson laugh even harder.

The bell above the door rings, and a couple holding hands walk in. They smile at us and say hello, and Mr. Johnson goes to help them. I don't have a chance to promise him a jar of my mama's chicken and dumplings, but it doesn't matter because I've already made the promise to myself.

"See you soon, Mr. Johnson," I call on our way out.

And with that, Jewel and I are fast-running, loud-singing, slow-skipping all the way to Mr. Inge's grocery store to get us some Mary Janes. And while I'm running, I can practically hear my Man-for-Mama Plan jingling like wedding bells, right inside my dress pocket!

seven
MILE-LONG MINUTES

That evening, I decide to wait for the perfect time to tell Mama about Mr. Johnson being back in Charlottesville, being single, and saying hello. So here I am, sitting on the floor with my back in front of Mama, who's sitting on Grandmama's chair, rebraiding my hair. And I'm finally spilling the beans.

"Do you remember a boy in your class named Odin Johnson, who used to tease you?"

"Odin Johnson," Mama says, while parting my hair. "Yes, I remember Odin."

"Is it true you used to kick him in the shins?"

"Who told you that? And why are you asking about him?"

"He's moved back to Charlottesville, and opened up Odin Johnson's Antiques. Jewel and I like to go inside and make up stories about all the old things in there."

"I declare!" Mama says, tugging my hair. "I saw the sign going up and wondered if it was Odin from my school days."

"And guess what?" I say, turning to see Mama, even though it makes my braid she's holding tug my scalp. "He's single!"

"Okay," Mama says with all the excitement that could fit

inside a thimble. "Now will you turn yourself around, please, so I can finish your hair?"

"Actually...there are quite a number of bachelors down on West Main," I say.

"How do you know that?" Mama leans over to look at me, which makes my braid tug at my scalp again.

"Jewel and I are observant, that's all."

"I don't know what you're up to, Alexandra Lewis, but instead of wasting time gallivanting around town making up stories and paying heed to who's a bachelor, I'd rather you check in with Miss Viola to see if she needs help pulling weeds from her flower beds. You know she's practically blind."

"I know, Mama," I say. "But trust me, we're not wasting time. Besides Miss Viola's weeds sometimes have pretty flowers."

"*Hmph*," is all Mama says as she goes back to braiding my hair.

The next morning when I get up, Mama has already gone to work, so I can't tell her anything more about Mr. Johnson. With Miss Greta fast asleep in Grandmama's chair, I decide to make some biscuits. Soon their buttery smell will begin dancing around this here house, and Miss Greta's nose will be waking her right up. That's how it is with Miss Greta. Her nose does a better job of watching me than her eyes do.

After I put six perfectly round biscuits in the oven, the soft rumble of Miss Greta's snoring comes into the kitchen to waltz with the sound of the kitchen clock's ticking. *Heee.*

Tick-tick. Woota-woota-woota. Heee. Tick-tick. Woota-woota-woota.

I set the table for Miss Greta and me and think about the ingredients I'll soon be sneaking over to Jewel's house so we can make sugar cookies to sell. It feels good to have my Man-for-Mama Plan chugging along full steam ahead, so I begin humming a happy song that suits the occasion. I hum while putting a clean cloth inside a bowl so I can wrap the biscuits to keep them warm when they're done baking. I hum while pouring the orange juice Mama squeezed out yesterday. I hum while getting the jar of honey we bought from Mr. Smith a few Saturdays ago.

Next to the honey, I place Grandmama's butter dish that holds several pats of butter with little bees stamped on them. I love to watch Mama use the wooden tools Grandpa made for Grandmama to make her butter pretty—two small paddles to make little balls of butter and a small butter stamp with a bee carved into the bottom. My mouth starts to water as I think about the butter pat, bee and all, that will soon be melting onto my biscuit.

But then—just as I'm taking the biscuits out—*Wooommpppp!*

Jewel flings open the back door that leads into our kitchen and flies in. She's holding a jar that's filled with dollar bills. Her face is red. Her tears are streaming.

I put the biscuits on the counter and run to Jewel. I grab hold of her hand and start to cry, even though I don't know why she's crying. What has happened?

Miss Greta appears in the kitchen. "What's wrong?"

"It's Gramps! He—he—he was lying there this morning. I

couldn't get him up. Dr. Stratton came. He and Mr. Bell took him to the hospital. I've got to make sure he's okay! Allie, will you come with me to the hospital?"

"Of course I will!" I say.

"I'll catch the streetcar to Mrs. McIntire's and fetch Allie's mother," Miss Greta says. "We'll be there as soon as we can!"

I throw on my shoes. And Jewel and I run toward the University of Virginia Hospital as fast as our legs can carry us. We run up Fourth Street NW, then down West Main Street, block after block—past Union Station, beyond the Queen Charlotte Hotel, and under the Fourteenth Street bridge, until we're finally at the hospital. We go in the basement entrance where the ward for colored people is located and run straight up to the lady who's sitting at the front desk.

Above the awful noise of sick people crammed into a small space, Jewel yells, "My grandfather! Is he okay? My grandfather—Oh, please, where is he?"

The lady at the desk looks at Jewel with kind eyes. "What's his name, darling?"

Through tears, Jewel wails, "Mr. Poindexter. Sydney Poindexter!"

"Sydney Poindexter...," the lady says, then she looks down a list. "Yes dear, your grandfather is here."

"But is he okay?" Jewel asks. "Tell me he's okay."

"He's in good hands," the lady says.

Jewel places her jar with dollar bills onto the lady's desk. "Please," Jewel says, "please give this to his doctor. Tell him to take care of my grandfather. Tell him he's all I've got in the world!"

The lady stands up and hands the jar back to Jewel. "Don't worry. Dr. Collins is on duty today. He'll take good care of your grandfather."

"Can I see him?" Jewel says.

"You'll have to wait for the doctor," the lady says, and she goes back to looking at the papers on her desk.

Near the door, on chairs lined up, Jewel and I sit down. There's a long, dark hallway to our right. It's filled with injured people lying on cots, moaning people sitting in chairs, all kinds of people needing help, with no privacy at all. The smell of sickness hangs everywhere. Water drips into a bucket from the pipes above. I even see a rat scurrying in the darkness! A rat!

My inside heat clanks like radiator steam trying to get out. What kind of hospital is this, treating good people needing help like they are less than human? Makes no sense. None at all!

"If that Dr. Collins doesn't take care of your grandfather," I loud-say to Jewel, "we'll write a letter to President Roosevelt!" And I hope the people upstairs sitting in their fancy in-charge offices hear me!

But Jewel, lost in her sea of tears, doesn't say a thing. She's hugging her grandfather's money jar like I hug Mitzy during a bad storm. Even though I want to pry her hand away to give it an it's-going-to-be-okay squeeze, I don't. I lean toward her and place my shoulder on hers. When I do, I feel Jewel's tears waterfalling down my arm. Mine start waterfalling, too.

After several long minutes, I start to wonder. Why doesn't the doctor come out to tell us what's happening with Mr. Poindexter? Is Mr. Poindexter okay? Is he...alive?

Ten minutes pass like ten hours. A little boy with his arm in a cast comes out, but the doctor doesn't come to tell us about Mr. Poindexter. Fifteen minutes pass like fifteen hours. A woman with a brand-new baby comes out, but the doctor doesn't come to tell us about Mr. Poindexter. Thirty minutes pass like thirty hours. A man with a bandage around his head comes out, but still, no one comes out to tell us about Mr. Poindexter. Minutes after minutes pass like hours after hours. *Please, oh, please,* I hard pray, *let Mr. Poindexter be okay for Jewel, my best friend in the whole wide world.*

At last, Mama and Miss Greta arrive! Sunlight streams around them as they walk through the open door. As soon as it closes behind them, the darkness of the basement gobbles the light. Mama takes one look at Jewel and marches up to the counter.

"Mr. Sydney Poindexter. I need an update immediately!" Mama says.

The lady looks down at her clipboard. "The doctor should be out any minute."

Mama stands tall just like the oak tree at Washington Park that belongs to Jewel and me stands, never breaking during storms. "We need to know his condition. Right now."

"Yes, of course," the lady says. "Hold on one minute." And she disappears down the hallway.

There are no empty chairs next to Jewel and me, so Mama and Miss Greta stand beside us. Jewel, with her jar of money now lying in her lap, grabs Mama's hand. And finally the minute arrives when the doctor comes out to tell us how Mr. Poindexter is doing. The doctor's white gown is stained. His pale white forehead is dotted with sweat. His blue eyes look tired. Seeing the doctor like that makes me feel like I can hardly breathe. I can tell he needs more help with all the folks in his care.

Please, oh, please let Mr. Poindexter be okay.

"Poindexter family?" the doctor says.

"Yes, sir," Mama says. "Right here."

The doctor walks over. Jewel and I stand up.

"Your father has had a mild stroke," he says to Mama as though she belongs to Mr. Poindexter. "But he's going to be okay. While I think he should stay overnight, he's insisting on going home. We'll be releasing him in a few minutes."

The doctor's voice is kind and he seems truly concerned about Mr. Poindexter.

"*OH!*" Jewel yells. "He's okay! He's okay!"

"He's okay for now," the doctor says, rubbing his brow. "But without proper care he could have another stroke and it might be worse. I strongly recommend he see a specialist who treats the heart as soon as possible."

While Mama and the doctor keep talking, Jewel and I stand there, pressed against Miss Greta and holding each other while we cry for what seems like hundreds—no, thousands—of mile-long minutes.

eight
A DAY FOR LUMPS IN THE THROAT

A few days later, Jewel gives me the terrible news. She and Mr. Poindexter are moving to Chicago, where Mr. Poindexter's sister, Jewel's great-aunt, lives. That way Mr. Poindexter can get good care at a wonderful hospital there called Provident run by colored people with physicians like Dr. Stratton who treat all their patients equally. Besides, Jewel's great-aunt had said, Jewel needs to be with her aunts, her uncles, and all of her cousins who live there—in case something worse than a mild stroke happens to Mr. Poindexter.

It's the right thing, I know, for Mr. Poindexter and Jewel to move to Chicago. But I don't want Jewel to go. I need her here with me! But today is Jewel's last day living in Virginia and my world is falling to pieces.

And so here I am, standing beside Mr. Poindexter's nephew's truck packed with Jewel's things, and I really want to kick that truck, because soon Jewel will be leaving inside it. I kick a rock instead and watch it skitter away toward Jewel's front yard, where Mr. Poindexter is selling all the things they didn't have room to take.

Mama and Miss Greta are in the yard, too, helping with

the tag sale. They're walking around with two jars, filling them up with money to help Mr. Poindexter with his medical expenses.

Mr. Poindexter is tipping his hat and saying, "Thank you very much for coming. I'll be missing you, too."

Jewel comes and stands by me. I feel a lump in my throat when Mrs. Bell buys Jewel's bed. I liked the way the springs squawked whenever we jumped on it. I feel two lumps when Mr. Carr buys Mr. Poindexter's gramophone. I liked hearing Billie Holiday sing whenever Jewel's grandfather played his only record. I feel three lumps when Miss Banks takes away Mr. Poindexter's teakettle and tea set. I liked the way Jewel and I put our pinkies up when we pretended to be sipping tea with the Queen of England.

But there's nothing I can do about it. Today is a day for lumps in my throat and knots in my stomach.

"You'll be all right without me, won't you?" Jewel asks when there are just a few things left to be sold.

"No," I say. "I won't."

"You still have Mitzy," she says.

"Mitzy's not real," I say.

"You'll have yourself a daddy soon," Jewel says, trying to smile.

"Without you, how can I make my Man-for-Mama Plan work?" I say. "Where will I bake the cookies? Where will I sell them? How will I make jars of chicken and dumplings and deliver them without you by my side? Who will help me pick the right man for Mama?"

"You can do it! We already did the hardest part talking to all those shopkeepers, and you've already got five red hearts on your daddy map. Five!"

I reach into my dress pocket for a piece of paper, but it's not my Man-for-Mama Plan.

"I made up a goodbye song for you," I say, handing her the paper. "I wish I had a flute so I could play it for you."

Jewel studies the paper that I've written music on. All around the music I've drawn the things Jewel and I like doing at Washington Park—swinging on the swings, imagining we're ladies-in-waiting, and daydreaming while sitting beneath our big old oak tree. Looking at the musical notes I've written, jumping long and slow on the scale, Jewel starts to hum the song.

When she's done, she says, "When I get to Chicago, and get my school saxophone, I'll play it every night!"

"I wrote it so you won't forget me," I say.

"I'll never forget you, Allie Lewis. Never." She hands me a piece of paper. "Here's my great-aunt's address. Don't forget to write."

And just like that, my bucket of tears starts leaking.

Mr. Poindexter comes over to us then. "Well, my dear," he says. "It's time for us to go. I'll miss you."

"I'll miss you, too," I say. "Please take care of yourself." And I give him a long hug.

Jewel rubs her wet eyes, then whispers in my ear. "When you get yourself a daddy, make sure he has a car so you can visit me, okay?"

Jewel slides into the truck followed by Mr. Poindexter.

The nephew starts the engine and begins to drive away. Jewel turns and looks at me through the rearview window. She's waving and waving, and I'm waving back. Even after the truck turns off the street that is now Jewel's used-to-be street, I'm waving. And just like that, my best friend is gone.

nine
CAESAR'S PLACE

After church the next morning, I write Jewel a letter.

> *Dear Jewel,*
> *I miss you already, though it's only been one day since we said goodbye. I will miss you when I start fifth grade. School will not be the same without you. Who will sit with me during lunch? What if I get mad at Gwen—who will calm me down? When you start your new school, will you write me and tell me all about it?*
> *I hope Mr. Poindexter is doing okay, and that you like living in Chicago. Please write back soon.*
>
> *Don't forget me.*
> *Your best friend,*
> *Allie*

Mama gives me a stamp to add to the envelope, and mails it for me on Monday morning, but it doesn't make me feel any better about Jewel moving. Even after Miss Greta makes me some sweet bread and serves it warm with wild blackberry jam on Tuesday afternoon, I'm not feeling any better. Even after Mama reads me my favorite poem by Paul Laurence Dunbar on Wednesday evening before turning off my lights—*Sleep, Love, and peaceful be thy rest. Good-night, my love, good-night, good-night*—I'm not feeling any better.

I can't seem to shake my Jewel-is-gone sadness.

By Thursday, Mama says she's sick and tired of me moping around this here house. So on Friday, while working at Mrs. McIntire's, Mama calls Aunt Lavern, asking if Uncle John will come by on Sunday after we get home from church to carry us over to their house for supper. And now here it is Sunday afternoon and Uncle John will soon be here.

"Can't we just stay home?" I beg. "I want to wash Mitzy's dress."

Mama wraps her apple pie in an embroidered tea towel. "If you wash Mitzy's dress one more time, it may turn to threads."

"You'd make her a new one if that happens, wouldn't you, Mama?"

Mama sighs an I-don't-know-what-I'm-going-to-do-with-you sigh. "Don't you want to see Caesar? It will help you with missing Jewel."

"There's no way on God's green earth Caesar can take Jewel's place." I feel my head shaking a little as I say it.

"Alexandra Lewis! No sassing me, you hear!"

"I'm sorry, Mama," I say. "I just don't want to go."

"We're going," Mama says. Then she looks out the window. "Your uncle John is here. Come along now."

I pick up Mitzy and start to slow-walk toward the door.

"Leave Mitzy here," Mama says.

"Oh please, Mama, let me bring her. I miss Jewel just a little less when I'm holding her."

Mama peers deep into me. "All right," she says. "But we're not going back to those days when you toted your doll everywhere you went. You understand me?"

"Yes, ma'am," I say, though I need to hold Mitzy right now, because I can tell it's going to take a while for the emptiness I'm feeling without Jewel to go away.

Mama leaves the house with her apple pie in hand, and I'm following.

"Afternoon, ladies," Uncle John says, holding the truck door open. He offers his hand, first to me, then to Mama, and we both squeeze in. Once he's behind the wheel, he asks, "Is that apple pie I'm smelling?"

It's funny, I think, how Uncle John can tell exactly what food my mama's made, even though it's inside a stove or underneath a lid or beneath an embroidered tea towel.

While we're driving toward Caesar's, I can smell mown hay and pine needles through the open window. When Uncle John rolls into Albemarle County the paved roads become lanes of dirt, and there are bales of hay in fields, hills of corn, and farmhouses staring down mountain views everywhere you look.

Albemarle County is where all four of my cousins were born—Caesar and his bossy sister, Jocelyn, who's a teen now; four-year-old John Junior, who we call "Chops" because he loves eating pork chops; and baby Judah, who we call Junebug because his buzzing-bubbles sound just like a June bug in flight. They were all brought into the world with the help of a midwife, right inside the same farmhouse where Uncle John grew up, which is the same one Uncle John's granddaddy, a freeman and a farmer, built a long, long time ago. Uncle John's grandaddy gave the farm to Uncle John's daddy, who gave it to Uncle John. And I suspect Uncle John will give it to Caesar, seeing how Caesar is his oldest son, unless Caesar decides he doesn't want to be a farmer.

When Uncle John turns down the lane that leads to his place, the truck *badump-badump*-bumps past apple trees loaded with apples. No sooner does Uncle John park the truck than Caesar comes running out to greet us. He pulls open the truck door on my side.

"Afternoon, ladies!" Caesar says, sounding just like his daddy, only Caesar's voice is lighter. "And how is my aunt Elizabeth doing today?" He holds out his hand for Mama.

"Just fine." She kisses Caesar on the forehead. "How's my nephew?"

"I'm fine as sunshine!" he says, which makes me laugh.

"How's my favorite cousin?" he says as soon as I jump out of the truck.

"Your only cousin is fine!" I say.

Seeing the pie in Mama's hands, Caesar sniffs like his daddy had sniffed. "*Mmmmm, mmm!* Is that apple pie?"

"Yes, sir," Mama says.

Walking toward the house beside me, he says, "I know *someone* who is going to *love* that apple pie."

Caesar's wide grin, one like the Cheshire Cat in *Alice's Adventures in Wonderland,* makes me wonder who on earth this "someone" is.

After Mama and Uncle John have gone inside, Caesar stops and looks right at me. "You doing okay, Allie Cat? I heard about Jewel."

Knowing Caesar will understand, I tell him, "I'm really missing her. It feels like my insides are broken to bits and nothing can be done to fix them."

Caesar puts his arm around me. "Is that why you have Mitzy?"

I nod my head.

"Don't worry," he says. "I'm right here."

"I can't run over here like I could run over to Jewel's."

"I know." He takes his arm away. "But when school starts, we'll see each other every day."

"What about Booker T.? When you're around him, you forget all about me."

"How could I ever forget my Allie Cat! Before school starts each morning, I'll wait for you at the bottom of the school steps. I promise."

"You will?"

"I promise, so I will," he says. "Now come on inside!

There's a great big caterpillar surprise waiting for you. And I know it's definitely going to cheer you up!"

"What kind of surprise?"

"You're about to find out!"

And all at once I'm thinking Mama was right about coming to Caesar's. I love surprises!

ten
SURPRISE, MY EYE

As soon as Caesar swings open his front door, there's a surprise all right!

My NOT-friend Gwen Turner is inside, sitting on my cousin's sofa! And just like that I feel my inside heat boil!

"UHHHHH!" comes fast-jumping out. And I turn myself around and run out of the house toward Caesar's climbing tree.

As soon as I get to the tree, I toss Mitzy on the ground, and fast-climb up its branches. I make my way to Caesar's sitting branch, quick-scooch over to where the branch meets the trunk, and press my back against the trunk as hard as I can. Only then do I realize I don't have Mitzy! I peer toward the ground and see her lying in a patch of red Virginia clay.

What was I thinking? Tossing Mitzy like that? But I'm not going back down to get her. Not yet. I have to get over the trick Caesar played on me!

Someone is going to love this apple pie!

Like I care if Gwen Turner likes my mama's cooking!

There's a great big caterpillar surprise waiting for you.

Like seeing Gwen Turner is a good thing! I could bop that Julius Caesar for making me think something good was about to happen!

"Stop your racket!" I yell to a bird *tweet-tweet*-singing above me.

And just like that, hot tears start flowing.

After a while, I stop crying, and start feeling hungry. Why hasn't anyone missed me, I wonder. Why hasn't Mama come out to see where I am? Where is Mama? I look toward Caesar's house and think on what to do, when I see Caesar coming outside. He's looking around for me.

First he spots Mitzy beside his climbing tree. Then he spots me up in his climbing tree. He waves, but I turn away, still mad at how he tricked me. Deep down, though, I'm glad to see him coming for me, glad to see him climbing to me, glad to feel him sitting beside me.

"Why'd you run off like that, Allie Cat?" Caesar says once we're leg to leg in his tree.

"You said there was going to be a surprise that would cheer me up. What kind of trick was that? You know full well how I feel about Gwen Turner! Seeing her would never cheer me up—not in a million years!"

"I know," Caesar says. "But Gwen is not the surprise."

"Oh? She isn't?" I feel silly now. "Then what's the surprise?"

"Mr. Coles."

"Mr. Coles, as in Mr. Coles our band teacher?"

"Yes, that Mr. Coles."

"How is Mr. Coles being here a surprise? He and your dad are always getting together."

"Here's the surprise part! A few weeks back, Mr. Coles saw your mama talking with Miss Greta at your church and he said a light bulb went off. So he called and asked my daddy to invite him over the next time your mama was coming for supper. I guess he was too nervous to ask your mama on a date directly. Or maybe he thought she'd say no."

"What are you saying? Mr. Coles is here to date my mama?"

"That's what I'm saying! That's the surprise!"

"And you thought that would make me happy like a surprise party? Have you got fluff where your brain should be? Mr. Coles is Gwen's uncle! He's not on my map!"

"Your map?"

"My plan."

"Your plan?"

"Never mind!" I say, because not only is my plan off track with Jewel leaving, but now Mr. Coles, uncle of Gwen, is trying to get his name mixed up in it!

"I don't know about any map or any plan," Caesar says. "But I do know this. You like Mr. Coles just fine. Never mind him being Gwen's uncle. You're always saying you wish your mama would get married again."

Deep down, if I had to admit it, Mr. Coles probably would check off some of the boxes I've got on my list. He has a kind smile. He definitely knows how to fix things. Like last year, he straightened the bar on my flute when I thought for sure it was beyond fixing. And boy, can he sing. He sang a solo so well at church one time, I thought he could be on the radio. But Mr. Coles is not the one for my mama! How could he be?

Might as well cover me in poison ivy if Gwen were to be my same-age cousin!

For as long as I can remember, Gwen has been my NOT-friend. Like the time in first grade when we all had to share our drawings in front of the class, and she said my horse looked like a penguin, and everyone laughed. Then afterward, she held up her drawing and everyone *oohed* and *aahed*, saying hers was amazing. Or the time in second grade when I was reading out loud and my mouth felt full of marbles, because I was still learning how to read. And I looked up and there she was staring at me like I was dumb. Then afterward, when it was her turn to read, her words came flowing out like she was born reading books. Or the time in third grade when she sat her box of sixteen brand-new crayons right next to my not-new box of eight. Then afterward, she held up her box for everyone to see and said, *Look what my daddy bought me!*

Or how about last year, when the worst thing ever happened. I'd gotten my borrowed flute for the school year and practiced and practiced my audition music before school started. And my audition went really well. Then afterward, who played better than me? Gwen Turner, that's who! All because her daddy had bought her a flute that summer, and she had been able to practice weeks more than me. That was the worst feeling ever! Like Gwen Turner had stolen—STOLEN!!—my chance at first chair!

Year after year, Gwen Turner has known exactly how to make me feel like I'm a great big nobody, while everybody believes she's the most amazing somebody! It's like she walks in and my chance of drawing a perfect picture is crumpled up and thrown away!

Just thinking on it makes jump-rope knots skip inside my

stomach. No way Mr. Coles, uncle of Gwen, is finding a spot on my map! He's NOT the one!

"I'd rather eat glass than be related to Gwen Turner!" I say.

"Well, that's dumb," Caesar says as he starts to climb down the tree. "Anyway, you better come inside. Mr. Coles might be talking all sweet with your mama at this very moment. Besides, I'm hungry."

Right away I start imagining Mr. Coles and Mama talking and laughing inside Caesar's house. And they're not talking about how I'm doing in band. No! They're talking because he's single and wants to date my mama! I've got to get out of this tree and into the house! And so I climb down as fast as a person can scooch. I grab Mitzy and run toward the house.

Caesar is there holding the front door open for me. With Mitzy behind my back, I go in.

I don't know how I missed seeing Mr. Coles in Caesar's living room, but sure enough, there he is, sitting next to Uncle John, who's all comfortable in his favorite chair. Thankfully, it's Uncle John that Mr. Coles is talking to, and not Mama.

"Hello, young lady," Mr. Coles says.

"Hello," I say, though I want to say *Go away, Mr. Coles, I only want to see you at school—in a few weeks—not here, not now.*

Gwen is still on the sofa. She's grown-up talking with Jocelyn about stockings, and they're ignoring me, which is fine by me. I stick Mitzy behind Uncle John's chair before Gwen has a chance to see her.

"Allie Cat!" says Chops, who's on the floor, playing with Junebug.

Junebug sputters a hello. *"Buzzuwuzza-zzz!"*

I give Chops and Junebug a kiss, then head to the kitchen to check on Mama.

Mama and Aunt Lavern have their backs to me and don't see me when I walk in. Mama is mixing butter into mashed potatoes, and Aunt Lavern is spooning hot buttered beets into a bowl.

I hear Mama say, "It's a shame his wife died."

Mama then sees me and stops talking.

"Allie!" Aunt Lavern says. "It's about time you came in here to give your auntie a hug."

Hugging Aunt Lavern is warm and soft.

"Are you talking about Mr. Coles?" I ask. "Did he have a wife who died?"

Mama hard-looks at me. "Haven't I told you not to butt in to adult conversations!"

"But Mama, I didn't butt in. I just came in."

Aunt Lavern looks at her sister and says, "Lizzie, it won't harm the child to know what we're talking about."

Mama rolls her eyes at Aunt Lavern. She doesn't like it when her sister gives her advice on raising me.

Aunt Lavern starts their grown-up conversation again, this time including me. "Mr. Coles's wife passed away while she was having their first child—a girl. Neither one made it."

"Oh," I say, now understanding why Mr. Coles treats Gwen more like a daughter than a niece.

"What did you come in here for?" Mama asks the question like I was on-purpose eavesdropping.

"I was wondering if you needed help buttering the rolls," I say, though I wasn't really.

Aunt Lavern says, "You can take the food to the table. Get Jocelyn to help."

When I walk back into the living room to get Jocelyn, I notice Caesar is sitting next to Gwen and telling her some fool joke. My inside heat starts rising. My cousin has obviously forgotten all the mean things Gwen has done to me over the years! What kind of brother-cousin is he? He's supposed to be on my side!

"How do you make an octopus laugh?"

"I don't know, how?" Gwen asks.

"With *ten-ti-ckles*. Get it?"

Gwen bursts out laughing. "Ten tickles—tentacles! Good one!"

"*Guhhhh!*" I hear myself moan out loud when Gwen starts laughing, which makes Jocelyn start laughing at me.

"It's not funny!" I say to Jocelyn. "Your mama said you and I need to bring the food to the table, so you better come on."

After everything is set out, Aunt Lavern says, "It's time to eat," and everyone else heads into the dining room.

Uncle John sits at the head of the table. To his left sits Aunt Lavern, then Junebug in his little chair, Jocelyn, and Chops. Caesar is at the other end of the table with Gwen next to him. And who am I stuck sitting next to besides Mama? Gwen Turner, my NOT-friend, that's who!

"Everything smells delicious," says Mr. Coles, to the left of Mama. He smiles and Mama smiles back.

After Uncle John says grace, I can hardly notice what's in

each serving dish we're passing around the table. The sweet tea might as well be milk, so I pour only a little. The fried chicken might as well be meat loaf, so I take only a leg. The beets might as well be unsweetened rhubarb, so I get only a spoonful. The mashed potatoes and gravy might as well be white rice without butter, so I pile only a tiny mound with barely any gravy. But I can't help but notice the buttered rolls, so I take three.

Once everything has been passed around, and all my family is talking at once, I find myself staring down the table, past Mama and right at Mr. Coles. I do not like the way he chews his food. I do not like the way he wipes his mouth with his napkin. I do not like the way he's talking to my mama like he's gone and forgot that I'm his student and Mama is my mama!

Why can't it be Mr. Johnson from the antique store, or Mr. Journey from the sewing machine shop, or Mr. Edwards the insurance man, or Mr. Goins the tailor, or Mr. Mills, who owns the dry-goods store that sells men's clothing, sitting next to Mama instead of Mr. Coles?

While I'm chewing on my chicken leg, I find myself accidentally staring at Gwen. Why can't it be Jewel sitting next to me instead of Gwen? After a forkful of beets, I find myself also accidentally staring at Caesar, who is still telling jokes to Gwen. Why can't he be sitting next to me, telling me jokes instead? He knows how sad I am about Jewel!

Mama must notice all my accidental staring, because she says to me, "Child, concentrate on eating your food before it gets cold!"

Caesar says, "Mr. Coles, did you know that my aunt Elizabeth makes the best chicken and dumplings in the whole wide world?"

And before I realize it, I'm aiming a fork at Caesar. "Why don't you put some food in that fool mouth of yours, Julius Caesar?"

"Allie!" Mama says.

"Sorry," I say, though I really do wish Caesar would quit jabbering his jaws about my mama's cooking!

I reach for a fourth roll. While I'm reaching—*oops*! My hand bumps Gwen's glass! It teeters. It totters, and—*splooshhh!*—iced tea spills all over Gwen, soaking her pretty dress.

"*Guh!*" Gwen yelps.

"I'm sorry," I say, looking at Gwen. "It was an accident."

Caesar stands up and hands Gwen his napkin, while Aunt Lavern quickly gets up and heads to the kitchen for some towels.

"I really didn't do it on purpose," I say to Mama's glaring eyes.

"You ruined my new dress!" Gwen says, looking more at her uncle and less at me.

"Now Gwen," Mr. Coles says, "the tea will probably wash out."

"Sorry," I say again.

Aunt Lavern comes back with two towels, one for Gwen to dry herself off, and one for mopping up the spill.

"I'll help," Caesar says, reaching for the towel.

"No," Mama says, "Allie will."

So I get out of my chair, take the towel from Aunt Lavern, kneel down, and start sopping up the iced tea that's under

Gwen's chair. While I'm on my knees, crouched beneath the table, I hear Gwen whisper, "You did it on purpose."

Though she can't see me, I shake my head, though I'm wondering... *Did I?* I don't think I did. Surely I wouldn't have wasted a perfectly good roll, now soggy in a puddle of iced tea.

After I'm done cleaning up under Gwen's seat, I head to the kitchen to put my ruined roll into the kitchen scrap bucket, wring out the towel, and wash my hands.

"Caesar"—I hear Mr. Coles breaking the silence—"did you hear the story of the time your dad and I were out there fishing on the Rivanna..."

"Don't tell that one!" Uncle John replies.

But Mr. Coles clears his throat and starts in on the story anyway. I guess he's trying to calm things down between Gwen and me.

After washing my hands, I stand in the entryway between the kitchen and the dining room. Gwen's eyes are fixed on her dress, and I think, though I'm not sure, they're wet with tears. I really didn't spill that tea on purpose. But part of me is glad that Gwen got what was coming to her, always making me feel like she's better than me. Though I know, I should pitch that gladness into the burn barrel just like it was trash.

I slip back into the living room where I hid Mitzy. I plop down on the sofa and pull her up to me. I close my eyes and start humming the goodbye song I made up for Jewel. Maybe, just maybe, the music will untie the knots I feel inside me. When I stop humming, I open my eyes.

There's Caesar, standing beside me.

"Nice song," Caesar says. "Kind of sad."

"I made it up, for Jewel."

Caesar sits next me. "Don't worry about Gwen. She won't stay mad about her dress. I'll make sure of that."

And I try hard to believe him, though if that tea stain doesn't come out, fifth grade may end up being my worst grade ever.

eleven
GREEN-EYED MONSTER

Once I'm home and my pajamas are on, I take out a piece of paper, a large book to have something hard to write on, and a pencil. I sit crossed-legged on my bed with Mitzy next to me and begin a new letter to Jewel.

> Dear Jewel,
> You won't believe this! Mr. Coles is trying to weasel his way into my Man-for-Mama Plan! He invited himself over to Caesar's house because he wants to date my mama!! He talked to her all during supper! GAG! Wouldn't it be just terrible if Gwen and I were cousins?!?! GAG times ten!! I'm going to change my Man-for-Mama Plan to speed things up. Tomorrow, I will cover all the red hearts on my map with black except for the one above Mr. Johnson's store. And instead of making cookies and selling them, and then buying enough ingredients for five jars of chicken and dumplings, I'm going to make one potful for supper and sneak a jar to Mr. Johnson when no one is looking. Then, once I know he likes the

chicken and dumplings, I'll get Mama into his store so Mr. Johnson can ask her on a date, they can fall in love, and get married.

Please write back SOON and tell me what you think of my new plan.

> I miss you.
> Your best friend,
> Allie

P.S. I'm also drawing the biggest, fattest, blackest heart a person can draw above Jefferson School tomorrow for you know who!
P.P.S. Do you have your own room?

No sooner do I fold my letter than Mama comes into my bedroom. She sits beside me. After a long stretch of her not saying anything, I'm wondering, is she thinking about what happened at Caesar's?

I can't help but break the silence. "Mama, I'm not in trouble for spilling that tea, am I?" I lean against her arm. "I didn't mean to knock it onto Gwen, honest, even if she thinks she's better than me."

Mama gives me that look—eyes meeting eyes—that tells me I probably let out a few more words than I should have.

"No, you're not in trouble," she says, "but this is exactly what I want to talk to you about. I do believe there's a green-eyed monster lurking nearby."

I laugh then. "There's no such thing, Mama. I know that."

"I'm serious," Mama says. "There is a green-eyed monster." Mama touches my chest, right where my heart is. "Right in there, and its name is Jealousy."

I usually don't feel inside heat rising when it's just Mama and me talking, but I feel it rising now, and my words come fast-tumbling out. "Who am I supposed to be jealous of?"

"Your mama notices things, you know, like how you might stare at someone and scrunch your nose at them like they smell bad, when all they're doing is laughing at someone's jokes."

"I'm not jealous of Gwen Turner, Mama! Not in a million years!"

"You sure about that?" Mama stands up.

"Yes, ma'am," I say. "I am absolutely, positively, certainly sure."

"That's good. But just in case the green-eyed monster should come calling, I want you to invite Love, the pink-eyed monster, over. The pink-eyed monster will send the green-eyed monster packing." She leans down, kisses me good night on the forehead, then whispers into my ear: "Sweet dreams."

"Sweet dreams," I say back.

After Mama turns off the light, I slip deeper under the covers with Mitzy. And I hope to have a sweet dream, one where no one named Gwen Turner is related to anyone named Alexandra Lewis.

On Monday morning, after Mama has gone to work, and Miss Greta and I have cleaned up the breakfast dishes, I head to my room to fix my map. I get out my tin filled with nubby crayons saved from previous school years, take out the black one, and color all the red hearts over with black, except for the one above Odin Johnson's Antiques. With only one red heart now above West Main Street, my map looks pretty drab. So I decide to decorate it.

First, at the top of the page, right in the middle, I draw the oak tree at Washington Park that Jewel and I claim. I fill its branches with leaves—little dots of light green. In front of the tree, standing side by side and holding hands, I draw a smiling man dressed in a suit and bow tie and a smiling woman dressed in a long, lacy white gown. All around the border of the map, I draw forsythia bushes blooming yellow, and redbud trees blooming pink. I draw bluebirds flying next to blue quarter notes.

When I'm done drawing, I look over my map. I thought it was perfect before, but now it really is.

I put my map, Jewel's letter (now inside the envelope Mama had left for me), and the three pennies Mama gave me for the stamp into my dress pocket and head downstairs.

Not wanting to have Miss Greta ask to check my spelling in Jewel's letter, I try my best to keep the stairs from creaking by tiptoeing, but the bottom stair *creeeeak*s anyway, and Miss Greta's eyes pop open.

"Child," Miss Greta says from her spot on my grandmama's chair. "Why are you creeping around like some burglar?"

"I didn't want to wake you," I say, which is pretty much the truth. "Mama said I could go to the post office to mail Jewel a letter."

"Oh," she says, closing her eyes again. "There no time for me to check your spelling. They take up the mail at noon. Well, go on."

And as quick as a rabbit, I'm out the door.

As I walk past the Andersons' place, my nose tickles with the smell of honeysuckle blooming. As I walk past Miss Viola's flower bed, I see butterflies getting their fill from the center of one-eyed yellow blossoms. As I walk past Mr. Charley's place, I hear him say, "Morning, Miss Allie." Then he wide-smiles as he always does.

"Good morning, Mr. Charley!" I say back.

Usually, I like to stop and listen to Mr. Charley as he tells stories about things that took place in his life during Slavery Times. Though he's ninety-two years old, his mind is as sharp as a tack. Some of Mr. Charley's stories make my inside heat rise. How dare Mr. Purcell treat Mr. Charley like he was an ox he owned rather than a man! But some of Mr. Charley's stories make my insides say—*Ha ha ha! Serves you right, Mr. Purcell.* Like how Mr. Purcell's horse named Napoleon that cost a fortune and won all kinds of cash-prize races would throw Mr. Purcell off his back, but always let Mr. Charley ride him. But I can't stop to hear his stories today. I've got a lot to do before Mama gets home.

After Jewel's letter is mailed, I plan on making Mama and Miss Greta some chicken and dumplings with enough extra to carry a jar over to Mr. Johnson. I sure was glad to see a chicken inside the icebox this morning! The tricky part of my plan will be sneaking out of the house before Mama gets home, and while Miss Greta is sleeping. I don't want either of them asking who the jar is for.

To save time, I start skipping toward the post office. While I'm skipping, I hear someone shout my name. I stop and turn toward the voice. It's Booker T., Caesar's best friend from school. What does he want? I wonder. He waves, then heads toward me, crossing the street just as the ice truck passes. I don't stop, so he just starts skipping beside me with a big silly grin planted on his face.

"Where you going?" he asks.

"To the post office," I say.

To save Booker T. any embarrassment from skipping beside me, I decide to fast-walk instead. Booker T. stops skipping and matches my pace. All the while, he's smiling and jabbering about the latest episode of *The Amazing Interplanetary Adventures of Flash Gordon* that he listened to on the radio.

"And you should've heard it!" he says. "Dr. Zarkov figured out how to make Flash invisible! He became the Avenging Shadow—"

"You know, Booker T.," I say, "Caesar might be my cousin, but I'm not in the least bit interested in Flash Gordon."

Booker T.'s smile fades. "You don't know what you're missing. How is Caesar doing, anyway?"

"Caesar is fine," I say. "I can't wait until school starts back when I can see him Monday through Friday."

"Me too. Did you hear we might not start school right after Labor Day?"

"Where'd you hear that? We always start school the Tuesday after Labor Day. Everybody knows that."

"Simon Bowles got polio, and a few county kids, too. That's why. They don't want more kids to get sick."

"Oh no!" I say, worried about Simon becoming paralyzed. "Are Simon's legs still working?"

"I don't know."

Now I'm wondering why Mama or Miss Greta didn't tell me about polio being here in our neighborhood, or about school not starting as usual.

"It's too bad about Jewel moving to Chicago," Booker T. says. "Is that why you're going to the post office? To mail her a letter?"

"You sure are nosy!" I say.

"Don't worry about Gwen when school starts back up. Since Jewel's not here, Caesar and I will referee so you and Gwen don't go head-to-head like Joe Louis against King Levinsky in the ring." Then he pretend-boxes the air.

I stop walking, face Booker T., and punch his arm. "What are you saying? I'm no fool boxer!"

Rubbing his arm he says, "You could've fooled me."

"Well, I'm not!" I start fast-walking again. "Don't you have someplace to go?"

"Actually...I do! See you!"

And just like that Booker T. stops walking beside me and starts running toward a streetcar on its tracks that's just about to pass. And what does Booker T. do? He jumps onto the back of the streetcar and holds on with all his might. I shake my head as he disappears down the hill. Though named after a very smart man, Booker T. must have a peanut where his brain is supposed to be. What if a police officer catches him flipping a streetcar, riding on the outside so he doesn't have to pay the fare?

Realizing I've wasted time watching Booker T., I run the rest of the way to the post office. Knowing about polio being in our neighborhood, I am all the more thankful that I can walk and skip and run.

twelve
DISCOMBOBULATED

As soon as I get home, Miss Greta shakes herself awake. "Gracious me, child! Enter like a young lady, not like a lumberjack!"

"Miss Greta, have you heard about school opening late or about Simon Bowles having polio?"

"Where'd you hear that?" Miss Greta says, rising from her chair.

"Booker T. told me. Is it true?"

"I haven't heard about children here getting polio."

"But what if I catch it?"

"Now, now... sit down. I'll fetch you some water."

Though I have a lot to do before Mama gets home, I decide to sit and cool off.

"Here you go," Miss Greta says, handing me a glass with little bits of ice scraped off the block of ice that's inside the icebox. "Let me make you a tomato sandwich. You look like a rag doll. Did you run all the way to the post office and back again?"

I nod my head for the back-again part as ice-cold water slips down my throat. Normally, Miss Greta would never let me sit on Mama's sofa while eating, but today she does, bringing me my napkin and my sandwich—sweet with garden tomatoes and mayonnaise—on a little saucer.

Miss Greta sits across from me in Grandmama's chair and fans herself. "I can see what Booker T. said has got you worried, but worrying won't change what may or may not happen. Your mama will help you cross whatever bridge you come to, if and when you come to it. Besides, if there's one thing I've learned from living, most bridges aren't half as bad to cross once you've come upon them."

I'm sure Miss Greta is right, so I decide not to worry about polio or Simon Bowles's legs, but to think only about getting a jar of mama's chicken and dumplings to Mr. Johnson before Mama gets home.

"Miss Greta," I say. "I'd like to fix chicken and dumplings for supper tonight, and I'm hoping you'll stay and have supper with us. That okay with you?"

"That sounds right nice. But don't expect me to clean up your mess."

"I'll clean up everything!" I say.

"Do you need my help?"

While it's true Mama normally does the chicken part of the chicken and dumpling recipe, I'm sure I won't need Miss Greta's help. I've watched Mama do it so many times I could probably do it with one hand. Besides, Mama has already cut the chicken into pieces.

"No, ma'am," I say to Miss Greta's offer. Then I take my saucer and glass to the kitchen, wash my hands, and get started cooking, ready to fill this here house with the smell of all kinds of deliciousness. And though I'll be the one making supper, it won't be a fib when I tell Mr. Johnson his jar is filled, not with my cooking, but with Mama's, because I'll be making it just like Mama would.

Once I've got the chicken simmering in the pot, I grab a clean mason jar from the pantry and tiptoe past a sleeping Miss Greta, seeing how I don't have permission to go into Mama's bedroom. Though I'm sneaking, I don't think Mama will mind if I use one small square of material from her wooden chest.

Not far down in the chest, I see a scrap from the dress Mama made me for second grade. How I loved that dress with its little flowers of red and blue! It'll make a perfect lid cover for Mr. Johnson's jar. I take it and quietly close the chest, and head to my room.

I open my little sewing box and take out my scissors. On the back side of the square, I draw a circle around the jar lid. I cut a bigger circle around the one I've drawn. The only thing I need now is a blue ribbon to tie around the jar. I know I won't find any extra ribbon in Mama's chest. She'd never waste ribbon by buying more than she'd need. The only piece I can think of is tying Mitzy's two braids together. And it's the perfect shade of blue.

Though I don't usually talk to Mitzy, I feel I owe her an explanation. "I know you'll look awfully plain without your ribbon, but it's for a good cause. It's for Mr. Johnson's jar of Mama's chicken and dumplings. I'm taking it over today. And if he has it for supper tonight, I'll be able to know by tomorrow if he loves it. And once I know that, then I'll know for sure he's the ONE for Mama. Then all I have to do is get Mama to go on over there, and BAMMO! They'll be falling in love and getting married. And surely Mr. Johnson will buy us spools of ribbon with yards to spare."

I tiptoe downstairs, hoping Miss Greta is still asleep. Sure enough, she is. I creep past her and hide Mr. Johnson's jar behind Mama's bread box in case Miss Greta comes into the kitchen. Then I go upstairs to draw until the chicken is ready and it's time to make the dumplings. When everything's done, I clean up the kitchen and fill Mr. Johnson's jar, put the lid and its cover on, and tie Mitzy's ribbon around the material to hold it in place, making a bow with the ribbon.

From the kitchen, I yell, "Miss Greta, I'll be back in a few minutes!" but I don't give her time to reply. I jolt out the back door, and start running with the jar toward Mr. Johnson's store. I only have fifteen minutes before he'll be closing up, and twenty-five minutes before Mama will be home. So I'm running as fast as my legs can run.

Right as I'm nearing his shop, I see Mr. Johnson outside, starting to lock up.

"Mr. Johnson!" I yell while running.

He looks toward me and waves, but must not think I'm running to see him, because he's walking away from his shop. So I yell again.

"Mr. Johnson, *waaiii—t!*"

And then, just then, I'm fast-falling on the sidewalk, and hard-hitting my head on it!

"OH NO!" I hear Mr. Johnson cry out.

"OH! NO!" I hear myself cry out because my jar has fallen, breaking to bits, spilling out Mama's cooking everywhere.

"Allie," Mr. Johnson is saying. "Are you all right?"

"I'm okay." I hold my head where it hurts. But when Mr. Johnson helps me up, the sight of West Main Street spins inside my head, which doesn't seem okay.

"Here," he says, handing me his handkerchief. "Press it on your forehead." His voice is kind. His eyes are concerned. "Are you able to walk all right?"

I try walking, and though my head hurts, the street is no longer spinning.

"I'm fine," I say, even though I'm upset over Mr. Johnson's broken jar.

"I'm going to walk you home. Just in case you get discombobulated."

I laugh when he says "diss-come-bob-you-lated," which makes my head hurt even more.

"But what about your broken jar?" I say.

"You're discombobulated all right. You were the one with the jar." He puts his arm out for me the way gentlemen do for ladies. "Don't worry about that. Let's get you home. Your mother is bound to be worried about you."

And so here I am, headed toward home, one hand on Mr. Johnson's handkerchief, pressing it down on my head, and the other holding on to the crook of Mr. Johnson's arm. Now I'm worried about the bridge I'll soon be crossing when Mama sees me with a bloody handkerchief on my head.

When we get to my house, I take Mr. Johnson up the front steps. I wish our front porch was as nice as Gwen's with two fancy white columns and railings all around. But at least I know our house is as clean as any run-down house can be.

Mr. Johnson knocks and Mama comes to the door. Miss Greta is on her heels.

"What's this!" Mama says, practically flying at me. "Are you all right?" She flashes an angry look at Mr. Johnson as if it was somehow his fault.

"I'm okay, Mama. This is Odin Johnson—he walked me home. I was discombobulated after I fell."

Mama takes the handkerchief away to examine my head, and without looking at Mr. Johnson, hands the handkerchief back to him. "Thank goodness you're okay!"

"I wanted to make sure she made it home safely," Mr. Johnson says.

"Thank you so much," Mama says, *really* looking at Mr. Johnson now.

"Of course," he says.

I can tell Mama is searching Mr. Johnson's face. Is she remembering that Odin Johnson who owns Odin Johnson's Antiques is the same little boy who used to tease her? Does Mama remember me telling her how I liked to visit Mr. Johnson's store? Mama must remember.

"Odin? Odin Johnson? Is it really you?" she says.

Mr. Johnson laughs. "Yes, it's me."

"It's been ages! How are you?"

"I—" Mr. Johnson tries to answer her, but Mama stops him.

"Oh, what am I doing? Don't stand in the doorway. Come on in and have supper with us! Allie made Miss Greta and me chicken and dumplings and there's a whole potful!"

"Why, thank you!" he says with a wide smile stretching across his face.

Miss Greta, standing as tall as I've ever seen her stand, says, "I'll get you a chair and set a place at the table."

Who knew falling on my head would practically call my plan done!

thirteen
BETTER THAN EXPECTED

With Miss Greta and Mr. Johnson downstairs, Mama uses a warm washcloth to clean off my forehead in the bathroom. I turn away from the sink, hating the sight of blood.

"Why on earth were you running down West Main Street this time of day?" Mama asks me as she opens the medicine cabinet.

Not able to come up with a made-up reason, I tell her the truth. "I was taking Mr. Johnson a jar of your chicken and dumplings. I wanted to get there before his store closed."

"*My* chicken and dumplings?" Mama opens the tin with the small bandages inside. "You did the cooking, not me."

"It's your recipe."

"It's not my recipe, it's your grandmama Louise's. You know that." When Mama presses the sticky part of the bandage over the scrape on my forehead, it pinches my skin. "I appreciate you wanting to be kind like that, but Alexandra Lewis, you need to be careful. I can't put you back in the oven to make you new parts."

"I'll be careful," I say as she places the bandage tin back

into the medicine cabinet. "But as you can see, I'm perfectly fine."

While Mama washes her hands, I lean against her. Her warmth makes me feel safe. "Thank you for inviting Mr. Johnson for supper," I say. "Once he tastes your chicken and dumplings, he'll forget all about being a confirmed bachelor."

Mama hard-laughs then, causing water to splash on my face.

"What's so funny?" I ask her. "I'm serious." It's not like Mama to laugh at me when I'm not meaning to be funny. I try hard not to let my inside heat rise.

"I can see that," she says. "But if Odin Johnson says he's a confirmed bachelor, one home-cooked meal is not about to change his mind." Mama is hard-laughing again. Why, I don't know. "Wash your hands, and while you do, let those romantic imaginings about marital status slip on down the drain."

"Why are you laughing at me? And what does 'marital status' mean?"

"Never you mind. Now come on. Your mama is hungry and she's looking forward to eating the food you cooked for her."

Mama leaves the bathroom and my thoughts turn into a tangle. Why did Mama laugh at me? What does "marital status" mean? And more importantly, why won't Mama call what's in the pot *her* cooking instead of mine? Mama doesn't understand how important it is for Mr. Johnson to love *her* cooking! And here he is, in our house, about to try *Mama's* chicken and dumplings, not Allie's! Romantic imaginings? Who's being romantic? My Man-for-Mama Plan is coming true! If Mama will just cooperate, this could be the day, the very day, that everything in my broken-down life will begin to mend!

"Well, there she is!" Miss Greta says all chipper when I come down with Mitzy. "It's about time!"

I slip into my chair and place Mitzy on my lap, knowing Mr. Johnson won't think I'm a baby for having her. After I scooch in my chair, I look over at Mr. Johnson. I can't believe it! He's actually sitting at my kitchen table and is kind-smiling at Mama, Miss Greta, Mitzy, and me! I can't wait to write Jewel and tell her!

"Will you say grace for us?" Mama asks him, and he does.

With my eyes closed, I imagine that from now on it'll be Mr. Johnson saying grace for supper. "Amen!" I say when he's done.

Miss Greta gets up, brings over the pot, and ladles each of our bowls with chicken and dumplings. When Miss Greta leans over and smiles at Mr. Johnson while ladling, I wish it were Mama leaning over him, smiling and ladling. And when it's Miss Greta and Mama and me laughing at Mr. Johnson's stories about growing up here, I wish it were just Mama and me here laughing. What is wrong with Miss Greta? Doesn't she realize she's old enough to be Mr. Johnson's mama?

No sooner does Mr. Johnson taste the chicken and dumplings than I know he likes them and I realize it doesn't matter who made them.

"Oh, my! This is wonderful! Thank you for inviting me!" he says.

"You're welcome," Mama says.

Mr. Johnson is soon asking for seconds, which fills me up with happy. In between slurps, Mr. Johnson tells Mama about his time away from Charlottesville. How he attended high school in D.C. and then Wilberforce University in Ohio. How he dreamed of becoming an engineer who makes factory machines safer. How he ran out of money after only a few years. How he ended up mopping floors in Baltimore, but how he saved and saved until he could move back to Charlottesville and open up his shop.

"Do you earn as much as if you were an engineer?" I hear myself asking out loud, though I didn't mean to.

"Alexandra Lewis!" Mama says. "It is rude to ask folks how much they make!"

"I'm sorry," I say, though I bet Mama wants to know as much as I do.

"I do okay running my antique store," he says. "Like my father always said, with hard work and thrift, anyone can get by, and have a little left over for a rainy day.

"How about you?" Mr. Johnson asks Mama. "What have you been up to, besides taking care of this beautiful young lady?"

Mr. Johnson leans in as Mama tells him about her life after eighth-grade graduation. How she married at eighteen. How her husband spent more time running away from his responsibilities than he did running toward them. How after he left home, she began working for Mrs. McIntire, who pays her well enough to take care of things.

All while Mama is talking, I'm studying Mr. Johnson's kind face. I'm listening to his warm words. I'm feeling his gentle ways reach across the table and lean against Mitzy and me. It's easy to imagine how wonderful my life would be if Mama becomes Mrs. Johnson. Then I'd have parents who love each other. Maybe I'd even have a little brother or a little sister. My map is right! Mr. Johnson is the ONE who will make it all happen! He checks all the boxes. He even loves my mama's chicken and dumplings.

No sooner is Mama done telling Mr. Johnson about the gown she made for Mrs. McIntire to wear to a fancy ball than Miss Greta, as bold as a summer sun, leans over, bats her eyes, and asks him, "So, what's a woman to do to wrangle you to the altar?"

Mr. Johnson starts coughing and Mama starts laughing.

"Greta!" Mama says, shaking her head.

But I'm very glad Miss Greta asked it. This is Mama's chance to see what she needs to do!

Mr. Johnson clears his throat. "Truth told, no woman has ever tried!"

"Mama! Did you hear that!" I hear myself saying out loud, though I had no idea the words were about to come out.

Mama looks at me like I've done lost my mind.

"Lord have mercy!" Miss Greta says. "Honey child, bring your fine self to church one of these Sundays and let the wrangling commence!"

Mr. Johnson wide-smiles while looking directly at Mama. "I just might."

Mama takes her napkin off her lap, places it on the table, stands up, and starts clearing the table. Miss Greta, Mr. Johnson, and I start doing the same.

"Mr. Johnson," I say, while walking dishes over to the sink. "Seeing how you ate two bowls of chicken and dumplings, am I right in assuming you *LOVED* my mama's recipe?"

"I did!" he says, placing his bowl and spoon into the sink. "I was just about to ask—" He turns toward Mama. "Lizzie, you wouldn't think me greedy if I took home a jar?"

"Not at all!" Miss Greta says before Mama gets a chance to say anything. "Let me ladle it up for you!"

"Thank you!" Mr. Johnson says, still wide-smiling at Mama. "You know, it just dawned on me. I do believe I could sell this deliciousness at my store. I could put up a display with a sign—*Mama's Chicken and Dumplings: A Homecooked Meal for the Unwrangled Man*. It sure would beat a can of beans! I'll buy the supplies. We'll split the profits. What do you think?"

"*The Unwrangled Man?*" Mama says. "*The Single Man* sounds better."

"*Single* it is," he says. "So Allie, are you up to making some more of your mama's cooking?"

"Yes, sir!" I say. "If Miss Greta helps me with the canning."

"I'm at your service!" Miss Greta is practically dancing as she hands Mr. Johnson his jar to take home.

"Is that okay with you, Lizzie?" Mr. Johnson asks.

"It's fine by me, if Allie and Miss Greta are up to it."

But since they're doing the work, they should get the profits, not me." And Mama wide-smiles right back at Mr. Johnson, which also makes me wide-smile, because I'm thinking pretty soon my pockets will be full of Mary Janes and happiness, too!

fourteen
JARS OF GOLD

It's a week later when, after hearing someone knocking, I open my bedroom window, peer down, and see Mr. Johnson!

I loud-say "Morning!" and he says "Morning to you!" right back. It's a great way to start a Monday. I quick-throw on my dress and jump down the stairs.

Miss Greta has already opened the front door, and Mr. Johnson is standing inside. At his feet, I see a full grocery tote and a box of twelve mason jars with lids. He's brought all Miss Greta and I will need for canning chicken and dumplings.

"I suspect," he's saying to Miss Greta, "it won't take long for the chicken and dumplings to sell out. William Jackson is painting a sign for me to put in my front window. It'll say: 'Mmmmm! Mmmmm! Warm your tum with a jar of yum! Mama's Chicken and Dumplings: A Home-Cooked Meal for the Single Man.' What do you think?"

Before Miss Greta says anything, I say, "I think you are very smart, Mr. Johnson! It sounds like a song!" Then I sing:

Mmmmm! Mmmmm!
Warm your tum
With a jar of yum!
Mmmmm! Mmmmm!
Get you some
Chicken and dummmplings.

Mr. Johnson laughs. "We may just have to record that for the radio!"

He pulls out one of the jars from the box then, and hands it to me. "What do you think of the label?"

The lettering of the label looks like olden-time writing, the kind people made when they dipped their pens into little wells of ink. It's fancy script that I can read, not quite cursive. MAMA'S CHICKEN & DUMPLINGS. Beneath the words is a line-swirl that looks like a whisp of steam that thins itself out, encircles the words, then traces out a bowl with a puffy heart above it.

"It's perfect!" I say, "Though a red heart would be better. Everyone knows red hearts mean something good. Black hearts not so much."

Miss Greta frowns at me. "Hush your mouth, child."

But Mr. Johnson sticks up for me. "You have a point, Miss Allie. I tell you what, if your chicken and dumplings sell, I'll make the next batch of labels with a red heart."

"Don't worry yourself one bit, Mr. Johnson," I say. "I can color these hearts in! No problem. I am an expert at coloring."

"Now you're talking like an entrepreneur!" Mr. Johnson says.

"A what?" I ask.

"An entrepreneur," Miss Greta says, "is a self-starting business owner like this fine gentleman standing before us."

"Miss Greta!" I say, hoping my frown will remind her of how old she is.

"I appreciate the compliment," Mr. Johnson says, opening the door to leave. "I best be getting along. Some folks from Ivy are coming by this morning with a lamp they want me to appraise, and I don't want to be late."

"Have a good day!" Miss Greta says. "Next time come on through the back door. It's always open for friends and family."

Hearing Miss Greta say that makes my inside-happy do a backflip! So I say, "Next time, come by on Saturday morning when Mama will be home!"

"How about Friday afternoon instead? I'd like to have the display stocked and ready by the time I open Saturday. That's when my store is the busiest. Will Friday, say around three, be too soon to pick up twelve jars of gold?"

"Not at all," Miss Greta says, batting her eyes. "Friday it is!"

"Next time after this time, make it a Saturday morning!" I say.

As I watch him walk away, I wonder if I can somehow convince Mama to come home early on Friday when Mr. Johnson plans on picking up our jars of gold.

fifteen
TINGLE-TANGLED MESSY FEELING

It's Saturday and Mama and I are out the door going back-to-school shopping in some of the bigger stores on East Main Street in Charlottesville. We're going to Tilman's, a department store, to buy fabric for my new winter coat, and then to Woolworth's to buy school supplies. After that we'll head back to my school so I can finally get a flute for the upcoming year.

As I think about seeing my band teacher, Mr. Coles, at the school in a few hours a tingle-tangled messy feeling grows inside me. On the one hand, I feel a happy tingle—the kind you get when the circus parade is marching through town. That's because I know that once I have a flute and the audition music I'll finally be able to practice for first chair! And with school not starting for two extra weeks because of polio, I should be able to catch up to Gwen, who's probably been practicing her flute all summer.

On the other hand, I feel an unhappy tangle—the kind you get when your hair is twisted into your rubber band and the only way to remove it is to cut it out. That's because I'm worried about Mama seeing Mr. Coles.

Mama seemed to have such a good time when Mr. Johnson stayed for supper last week, but she hasn't mentioned him since. It's like she's plumb forgotten all about him, even though I've tried and tried to get her to remember the perfect supper we had. And this morning, when I suggested we walk by his store to see the chicken and dumpling display on our way to do our school shopping, she said no, we were cutting through our neighborhood like we always do. I think Mama is remembering her supper with Mr. Coles at Caesar's house rather than remembering her supper with Mr. Johnson at our house. I believe she's got seeing Mr. Coles on her mind, and that's why she's missing out on her chance to see Mr. Johnson today.

Maybe, just maybe the chicken and dumplings will sell out today and Mr. Johnson will come by with more supplies after Mama and I get back home. Maybe he'll even come by when I'm practicing my flute, and Mama will invite him in for his very own concert.

As we near Tilman's, I see one of those signs—*No Colored Allowed*—in a shop window, which makes my tangle yank harder inside me. Makes no sense. None at all. The skin of every human being has some kind of color. A person would be invisible if not. But Mama doesn't seem bothered by that sign. She just walks right past it like the owners of that shop don't need her hard-earned money anyway. Tilman's doesn't have such a ridiculous sign in its storefront window. We could even go to see a movie at the Paramount if we wanted to. All we'd need to do to see *She Gets Her Man* is pay thirty cents, fifteen for me and fifteen for Mama, use the side door entrance, and sit in the balcony. Of course, the only time Mama would ever spend her money on anything like seeing a movie is during winter break. Like last year, when we met Aunt Lavern and my cousins at the Paramount to see *Babes in Toyland* with Laurel and Hardy. It was hilarious, worth every penny!

When we go inside the department store, the bell above the door rings, and the lady behind the counter smiles at us. We smile back, then head over to the wall that's full of all kinds of fabric for sewing all kinds of clothes and curtains and furniture coverings. Mama walks to the fabric for making wool coats.

"Do you like this color?" Mama asks as she runs her hand over gray fabric.

I start to itch just looking at it. "I'd rather have a coat from the Chicago Mail Order Co. catalog," I say before realizing I've said it.

Mama stops looking at the fabric and glares at me like I'm being ungrateful.

So I say, "The pretty pink fabric near the top doesn't look so itchy."

"Pink is impractical for every day," Mama says to me. Then she asks the lady to cut the itchy, dingy-gray fabric that Mama has obviously picked out, no matter if I like it or not.

While the lady cuts the fabric, I stare out the storefront window, trying hard to be grateful for the coat Mama will make me. After all, the coat she made for me two years ago was cut from an old lady's coat she got from the secondhand clothing store. I was so glad when I tried that thing on yesterday and wasn't able to button it.

When I hear Mama ask the lady behind the counter for a yard of black ribbon as shiny as just-polished shoes, I feel myself smiling then, because I know Mama will add it to the collar.

"Thank you, Mama!" I say. "I won't look like a little old lady now," which makes the woman behind the counter laugh.

The lady wraps my new coat fabric and ribbon in brown paper, and ties it up with string. Then she hands me a wooden nickel that says it's worth five cents, but I know full well, the only place to spend it is here, and Mama and I won't be back for a good while. So as we're walking out and another mama and her little girl are walking in, I hand her the nickel.

"Thank you!" the girl says, and her mama smiles at me.

Mama lets me hold the package, which makes me feel like I'm thirteen instead of ten and we head to Woolworth's to get my school supplies: a box of crayons, pencils, an eraser, and a jar of rubber cement.

"Mama," I say as she places my supplies on the counter to purchase them, "may I have a Moon Pie? Please?" I sigh when she says no.

"Be grateful, child, for what's in your bag." And I try to be.

After Woolworth's, Mama and I begin walking back toward Vinegar Hill and my school. With each step closer to my flute, I'm praying Mr. Coles will not flash some fool smile at Mama, and Mama will not flash one back at him.

When we're almost there, I tug on Mama's arm.

"Yes, Allie?" she asks.

"Will you please remember Mr. Coles is my band teacher, and nothing more?"

"Nothing more," Mama says with a teasing-you tone in her voice. "Not a man. Not a person. Not a human being. Just a band teacher. I'll remember."

"I'm serious, Mama!"

"So am I."

"It's Mr. Johnson you should get better acquainted with—not Mr. Coles." I hear myself almost shouting. "How can you forget our perfect supper? How can you ignore that he's the one selling your chicken and dumplings? How can you ignore the fact that he's the one?"

Mama stops walking and looks at me, one eyebrow in the air like I've grown an extra head. "What did I tell you? Stop filling your head with silly notions!"

Then we start walking again.

I just don't understand Mama. My notions aren't silly! If I were imagining that Mrs. McIntire had bought me a silver flute from France—now that would be a silly notion! But if Mama starts smiling at Mr. Coles like she did at Caesar's house, then—*BOOM!*—everything I've got planned for her and Mr. Johnson will fall apart. That's not a silly notion. It's the truth!

But it's too late now. My tingle-tangled feeling has grown into my throat, and it's making my heart play staccato beats—faster and faster as Mama and I walk up the steps of my school. If Mama only knew how fast my heart is beating, how big my throat lump is getting, how high my inside heat is rising at the thought of her seeing Mr. Coles again instead of Mr. Johnson, then I'm sure she'd be taking this moment we're walking down the hallway toward the band room way more seriously.

The line outside of the band room is slow-moving toward Mr. Coles, and I'm glad. In front of us are Lorinda with her parents. She plays the clarinet. Also in line are Alma and Pearl, the twins. They play the flute, too, but not very well. Samson is also there with his father. He plays the saxophone like Jewel. I know I won't see Caesar or Booker T. today, because they both play in the percussion section, and drum players don't get their own instruments to take home. They can practice on anything, be it a bucket or a chair arm. Caesar's favorite instrument is the snare drum. That's why Uncle John bought him his own set of drumsticks.

As the line moves toward Mr. Coles and our instruments, Mama and Lorinda's mama talk about a hurricane that's brewing out in the Atlantic, and how they hope we don't get bad rains here, this far inland. Mama asks how Simon Bowles is doing, and Lorinda's mama says Simon is on the mend, and his legs are working fine. Right as my mama tells Lorinda's mama to send Mrs. Bowles her love, it's my turn to pick up my instrument.

"Elizabeth!" Mr. Coles says all chipper, as soon as he sees Mama.

"You mean Mrs. Lewis," I say, but Mr. Coles does not correct himself, and takes Mama's hand and long-shakes it.

"Good to see you again!" he says to Mama, ignoring me, his student!

With her hand still shaking his, Mama says, "It's good to see you, too."

"Mr. Coles," I loud-say, hoping to break up this fool hand-shaking business, "you can assign me my flute now, and we'll be on our way."

Mr. Coles lets go of Mama's hand and picks up a flute. He checks the number that's inside the case, writes my name on the instrument-loan sheet, then hands Mama my flute, saying, "I wanted to call you—"

"We don't have a phone," I say.

"I realized that..." Mr. Coles hands me my audition music. "I'm wondering—I'm hoping—I'd like to—" Mr. Coles is stammering like he's forgotten how to speak English!

So I butt in: "You'd like to say goodbye, so I can start practicing!"

"Miss Lewis," Mr. Coles says to me, using my proper school name, "that's wonderful that you want to start practicing." Then he goes right back to talking to Mama. "There's a swing band playing at the red barn tonight. There'll be dancing! Would you like to come?"

"No," I say. "She's busy."

But Mama's reply is louder. "Yes! I'd love that."

And then, just then, I drop my music.

"Great!" I hear Mr. Coles say as I pick it up. "See you around eight?"

"Eight it is," Mama says.

And just like that all I want to do is run, run away from this here band room, run away from this school, run away from Mr. Coles, because Mama is not cooperating with my Man-for-Mama Plan! Obviously drawing a black heart above the school was not enough!

"Mama!" I say to her as soon as we're back outside. "You promised you'd think of Mr. Coles as only my band teacher!"

"No, I did not."

"But you don't even like dancing!"

"Yes, I do."

"But what about Odin Johnson who used to tease you?"

"What about him?"

"If you're going to go out dancing with someone, it should be with him. Not with Mr. Coles. Don't you know he's Gwen's uncle?"

"Yes, I know."

"Then how can you go on a date with him?"

Mama stops walking. She looks at me, smiles, and says, "Because I like him."

Because I like him? That's all Mama has to say? *Because I like him.*

Does Mama even take ten seconds to try to understand how awful I would feel if my NOT-friend Gwen Turner ended up in my life outside of school, laughing at me the way she does when I'm inside of school?

No.

Does Mama even take five seconds to try to understand how terrible I would feel if Gwen was sitting beside me outside of school making everyone believe she is perfection walking while I'm just a broken-down nobody?

No.

Does Mama even take one second to try to understand how horrible I would feel if Mr. Coles was her husband and Gwen Turner was my same-age cousin?

No.

Mama does not try to understand me.

If Mama did try to understand, then surely she'd never

have flashed that dumb, wide smile at Mr. Coles, but would have gone to Mr. Johnson's store to see the display and given him a wide smile instead.

Because I like him!

Hearing Mama's not-trying-to-understand Allie's words echoing around inside my head makes my inside heat rise again, and I can't help but mad-march myself all the way home.

sixteen
NO SWEETNESS INSIDE

The minute we get home, Mama says to me, "You best check that attitude at the door, young lady, or you'll be spending the night in your room."

But I've already decided. I'm stomping up the stairs and shutting me and my attitude in my room until it's time for supper.

I stomp up. *BOOM! BOOM! BOOM!*

I slam the door. *WHUUUPPP!*

I throw everything down onto my bed, even my flute! *KWUMP!*

When I do, Mitzy topples and falls to the floor. *WUNK!*

"Don't look at me like that," I say to her, though I know full well her eyes can't see. "I've got to fix my plan, and you can't help at all! I wish Jewel was here!"

I take my map and part two of my plan out of my dresser and lay them down on my bed. I *think-think-think*. What can I do so Mr. Coles will never ask Mama to go dancing again? After a while, I turn over Part Two, and quick-write down my new step.

Ha ha ha, Mr. Coles!, I think as I look over my new step. *My Man-for-Mama Plan is coming for you!*

I tiptoe down the stairs, careful on the one that creaks, and peek into the kitchen. Mama isn't there so I look out the window and see her outside taking clothes off the line. I hurry into the pantry and take out a jar of chicken and dumplings that Mama canned a while ago.

I open the jar. *Tssssskkkk* it seems to say to me, like I'm up to no good.

"*Shhhh,*" I tell the lid as its seal releases from the jar.

Quickly, from Mama's wooden shelf of spices I take down three little jars—one with cayenne, one with paprika, and one with red pepper. Into the jar I start shaking. I *shake-shake-shake* cayenne in. I *shake-shake-shake* paprika in. I *shake-shake-shake* red pepper in. I shake into the jar as much of those hot-on-the-tongue spices that I dare to shake. I quick-put the lid back on the jar, screw it on tight, and shake it all up.

Just so Mr. Coles knows this is Mama's cooking, I run to my room to make a label. First, I cut a piece of paper, shaping it like Mr. Johnson's label. On the label I write "To Mr. Coles—My Mama's Cooking. TASTE IMMEDIATELY." Above the words I draw in a black heart. I put rubber cement on the back of the label, run downstairs, and stick the label onto the spiced-up jar of chicken and dumplings. I put the jar on the counter so Mama will for sure see it's for Mr. Coles, and give it to him when he comes to pick her up.

I feel a fat grin stretch across my cheeks.

I'm hoping that once Mr. Coles takes the jar home, heats the contents up, and tastes it, he'll think to himself, *I thought*

Allie's mama could cook, but boy, was I wrong. And then he'll forget all about dating Mama, and Gwen will never be my same-age cousin. After all, doesn't the *Ladies' Home Journal* that Miss Greta is always quoting say "A way to a man's heart is through his stomach"?

Now that my plan is back on track, I head upstairs to practice my audition music so I can not only catch up to Gwen's playing, but play better than her. First-chair flute, here I come!

After putting my flute together, I warm up by playing scales. I don't even need the sheet music to know which notes to make sharp or which to make flat or which to keep natural. From memory, I play the lowest C to the highest C, three octaves wide.

After the scales, I take out the audition music, study the key signature, study the notes, and let the song beat out in my head. Then, I place the flute up to my lips and play it for the first time. The note changes are going to take some time before I can play them perfectly, but I'm ready to work for what I want. So I decide I'm going to keep practicing until Mama calls me for supper.

After I've practiced the piece about fifty times, my stomach grumbles. When I listen carefully, I don't hear Mama working in the kitchen. After I've practiced the piece about a hundred times, my stomach grumbles and growls. When I sniff the air, I don't smell chicken frying. I don't smell anything coming from the kitchen. Why isn't Mama fixing supper?

After I've practiced the piece a million times, not only

is my stomach double-grumbling and double-growling, but my arms are tired from holding my flute up to my mouth. My fingers are tired from up-and-down moving above my flute's keys. And my lips are tired from *tah-tah-tah-*blowing all those notes over and over and over again. Still, when I sniff and listen, I know for sure that Mama has plumb forgot about feeding me, all because she's going out dancing!

"See!" I say to Mitzy. "Mr. Coles is definitely wrong for this family! I guess I'll just have to go downstairs and boil myself some eggs!"

After cleaning and putting away my flute, I head downstairs. Like I figured, there's no supper on the stove, no supper in the oven, no supper on the table!

I jump when Mama, from behind me, says, "It was nice hearing you play your flute."

"Oh...*uh*...thank you...," I say.

"You're awfully jumpy," Mama says.

"I am?" I say, looking at the jar I fixed for Mr. Coles. "I guess my empty stomach has gone and made me agitated."

Mama says, "I made you a turkey sandwich."

She opens the icebox and takes out a plate with the most beautiful turkey sandwich! Lettuce and tomato are spilling out the sides. How I love turkey! Mama has put orange slices on the plate. How I love oranges! And she's put a pickle on the plate, and a pile of salty potato chips. How I love pickles and potato chips!

"Thank you!" I say.

"Sorry it's nothing hot."

"You bought potato chips and an orange just for me?"

"Just for you," Mama says. "The turkey is leftover from Mrs. McIntire's. I hope you like your supper."

In between bites of sandwich I say, "I'm sorry about slamming my door earlier."

"I know you are," Mama says, wiping the counter. That's when she nods at the jar I left for Mr. Coles. "It was very sweet of you to give Mr. Coles some chicken and dumplings."

I feel my neck and cheeks get warm, because I know I didn't add sweetness to that jar, only hotness.

But before I have a chance to confess, Mama says, "I've got to wash up and change now. Miss Greta will be here soon. When you've finished eating, clean your plate and get ready for bed."

"Yes, ma'am," I say.

Mama kisses the top of my head, and walks to her room with Mr. Coles's jar.

And so here I am left sucking on a sweet orange slice wishing I could go back in time and unshake those hot spices now floating inside a jar for Mr. Coles. But of course I can't go back in time. I could go into Mama's room and tell her what I did and why, but imagining how disappointed she will be keeps me from telling her, even though I know full well I should. Then a wonderful thought comes to me, one that does not involve me telling Mama what I've done. Since Mr. Coles is the wrong mister for Mama anyway, he's going to take one sniff of the spicy chicken and dumplings and throw the jar away without even trying what's inside so Mama will never know.

seventeen
SPYING

After washing my hands, feet, and face, after brushing my teeth, after putting on my nightgown and wrapping a scarf around my hair, I decide to write to Jewel.

I need to tell her about Mr. Johnson coming over for dinner. Tell her how he's selling Mama's chicken and dumplings at his store. Tell her how Mama said yes to Mr. Coles when he asked her if she'd go dancing with him. Tell her how I added hotness to Mr. Coles's jar. Tell her how Mama is not understanding how my insides will feel like a broken-down sidewalk with weeds in the cracks if I end up related to Gwen Turner. I need to tell Jewel everything, because no one understands me like Jewel, not even Caesar.

For some reason, and I don't know why, by the time I've signed my name to Jewel's letter, I've got tears spilling down my cheeks and they're crinkling up the paper. I take a deep breath to stop them and then blow my nose on my handkerchief. Then to add something happy to Jewel's letter, I get another piece of paper and draw her a picture of how I imagine Mr. Johnson's storefront looks with his Mama's Chicken and Dumplings display. In my drawing, on each jar, I add a label. Around each label, I draw golden-colored dumplings.

Above each jar, I draw a beautiful red heart. When I'm done, I fold the letter and drawing together and place them on my dresser.

I slip under my covers, pull Mitzy close, and wait for Mama to come and kiss me good night. But for the longest time, Mama doesn't come up. Even after I hear a knock on the back door, and then Miss Greta's voice, Mama doesn't come up. Even after I hear another knock, this time on the front door, then hear Mr. Coles's voice, Mama doesn't come up.

Mama may have made me supper, but she's forgotten about kissing me good night! Quiet as a mouse, I get out from under the covers and soft-open my door. I tiptoe down five stairs, just far enough to see through the railings and into the living room.

I spy Mr. Coles, not looking at all like my band teacher, but more like Duke Ellington, the musician. He's got on a suit I've never seen before. His hair is wavy and shiny like I've never seen before. And he's holding a walking cane! What on earth does he need a walking cane for?

I spy Mama, not looking at all like Mama, but more like Josephine Baker, the dancer! She's got on a sparkly red dress I've never seen before, red high-heeled shoes I've never seen before, and she's holding a red clutch bag I've never seen before. Why on earth is she wearing lipstick? Her lips are red enough!

"*Uhhhh!*" I hear myself groan out loud, though I wasn't meaning to.

Mama looks over and sees me on the stairs spying. Mr. Coles looks over and sees me on the stairs spying. Miss Greta looks over and sees me on the stairs spying. And so I run up the stairs as fast as I can, shut the door behind me, and bury myself beneath my covers.

Will Mama come up now and kiss me good night? Or will she come up to give me an earful for spying? Will she come up at all?

Mama doesn't come! I hear her saying goodbye to Miss Greta. I hear her shutting the door. I hear her leaving me behind while she goes out with Mr. Coles dressed like she's ready to be in a movie.

As soon as I hear the door shut, I jump out of bed, pull my chair next to my window, plop my knees on the chair, and look out. I'm just in time to see Mr. Coles opening the front door of Gwen's daddy's car for Mama, and Mama getting in.

And what is Mr. Coles holding besides his cane? The jar of chicken and dumplings I fixed hot especially for him. My eyeballs feel like they're going to fall plumb out, but I keep staring, even after Mr. Coles has driven away with Mama.

Pretty soon, the moon, looking like a squinty eye, pops over the line of trees on the other side of the street, and I'm pretty sure it's spying on me. But I don't care! I'm not leaving this window until I see Mr. Coles bringing Mama back home.

But when I open my eyes, I'm not at the window, I'm in my bed with Mitzy, and waking up to the smell of bacon. How did I get into bed? Did Mama ever kiss me good night? What time did she get home? Not remembering a thing after setting up camp in front of the window, I run downstairs.

"Mama! What time did you get home?"

"Good morning, sleepyhead. How would you like your eggs?" is all she says.

"Why did Mr. Coles take you in Gwen's daddy's car? You could've walked."

"We drove by Odin Johnson's Antiques last night. The display of your chicken and dumplings looks right nice, and it looks like he's sold some."

"Is that why you took the car? To see the display?"

"How about scrambled eggs with cheese?" is all she says.

"When you got home, did you come up to kiss me good night?"

"How else do you think you got in bed?"

"Next time you put on your red dress, why don't you go out dancing with Mr. Johnson?"

Mama takes the pan off the flame. She comes over and places her hands on my shoulders. "Listen, here, my little sunshine bee, mind your own beeswax. Not another word about this. You understand me? Not one."

"But—but—"

"Not one. Now wash up for breakfast before your eggs get cold."

eighteen
MESSED-UP SUNDAY

Later, after breakfast, Mama looks like Mama should as we walk hand in hand toward First Baptist Church on the corner of Seventh and West Main. Her hair is pinned up—not all shiny-curled and out. Her dress is plain gray and just below her knees—not all red and sparkly and down to her ankles. Her shoes are simple with a square heel—not all pointy and miles high. And her lips? Thank goodness! There's not a hint of red lipstick anywhere.

When we're about fifteen minutes from the church, I can't help but ask, "Mama? Where'd you get that dress you were wearing last night? I don't recall ever seeing it before."

"What did I tell you?"

"But I'm just asking about your outfit. That's all."

But Mama doesn't tell me where she got the dress.

When we're about ten minutes from the church, I can't help but ask, "Mama? Why on earth was Mr. Coles carrying a walking cane. Kind of strange, if you ask me. His legs work perfectly fine."

But Mama doesn't tell me why Mr. Coles had a walking cane.

When we're about five minutes from the church, I can't help but ask, "Mama? How much did that lipstick cost? Because I could sure use some more stamps."

But Mama doesn't tell me how much the lipstick cost.

When we're about one minute from the church, I can't help but ask, "Mama, why did you have to go dancing with Gwen's uncle? Why?"

Mama stops walking. She leans down, and eyeball to eyeball says, "Do you want to spend your afternoon writing out 'I will mind my own business' one hundred times?"

"No, ma'am."

"Then stitch your lips. You will not be warned again."

And I stitch them. Not because I don't want the answers to all my questions, but because I don't want to dull my new pencils by writing a sentence one hundred times, a sentence that is entirely wrong!

Mind my *own business?* Isn't Mama's business also mine?

If Mama goes out dancing with Mr. Coles, but forgets to kiss me good night, isn't that my business, too? If Mama fixes me a cold turkey sandwich instead of a plate with hot turkey and gravy over mashed potatoes, just because she has to get all dolled up, isn't that my business, too? If Mama keeps dating Gwen's uncle, instead of dating Mr. Johnson, isn't that my business, too? How can Mama not see that her business and mine are stitched together like two pieces of fabric? Mama should know that!

Mind my own business! That's exactly what I'm doing!

I try to calm myself down. Church is no place for getting

on Mama's bad side by fussing and arguing with her. I'd hate to be pulled outside by the ear with all the eyes of Vinegar Hill watching.

Once we're inside, two stained-glass windows light up the space, and I look around to see where Mr. Coles is sitting. I'm glad he's in the front row, which is already filled with people, leaving no room for Mama and me. Mama chooses a place for us to sit, and we scooch in. Today we end up sandwiched between the Andersons and the Mitchells. I'm glad Mrs. Anderson's arm is pillow-soft, because last week I was stuck with Mr. Fulton's hard elbow in my side the entire morning. I need a little softness this morning.

Pretty soon, Pastor Williams is thumping his Bible. Then the choir with Miss Greta in her white robe sways and sings "Lift Every Voice and Sing," and the congregation sings along. Once it's sung, the deacons pass the collection baskets. I drop in the pennies Mama gave me, then bow my head and say a silent prayer: *Please, Lord, make my Man-for-Mama Plan work. Put it in Mama's heart to like Mr. Johnson instead of Mr. Coles.*

When the service is over, Mama and I make our way through the crowd to the two large wooden doors that lead out of the building. As we're exiting, I can't believe what I'm seeing!

Down at the bottom of the steps are two misters looking straight at Mama! On the right is Mr. Johnson! He's tipping his hat and wide-smiling at Mama. On the left is Mr. Coles! He's tipping his hat and wide-smiling at Mama. I quick-look at Mama's face, and I can tell she doesn't see either mister. I watch as each mister, hat in hand, walks toward Mama.

Just as Mama and I step down the last church step, Mr. Coles is saying, "Morning, Elizabeth," at the exact same time as Mr. Johnson is saying, "Morning, Lizzie!"

Mama fast-blinks while looking at both of them. Mr. Johnson fast-blinks while looking at Mr. Coles. Mr. Coles fast-blinks while looking at Mr. Johnson. While I'm fast-blinking, I'm looking to see if maybe my prayer is about to be answered, and Mr. Johnson will fight for Mama just like men do in the movies, and Mama will be so impressed, she'll choose the right mister to marry! But fists do not start flying, only question marks soar above each mister's head.

Mama breaks the awkward silence. "Good morning. Odin, I'd like you to meet Raymond Coles. Raymond, I'd like you to meet Odin Johnson."

"How do you do," they both say, much too polite in my opinion, though I do think they're sizing each other up.

Mama says to Mr. Coles, "Odin and I went to Jefferson School together, same class from first through eighth grade." Then she says to Mr. Johnson, "And you remember my older sister, Lavern, don't you?"

Mr. Johnson nods his head.

"Raymond grew up in Union Ridge in Albemarle County near Hydraulic Mills. He went to Albemarle Training School with Lavern's husband, John."

I tug on Mr. Johnson's coat to tell him the most important information Mama is leaving out. "Mr. Coles here is my band teacher. That's all."

And I'm glad I shared it, too, because I can tell Mr. Johnson likes what I just said.

"Oh!" Mr. Johnson says. "Nice to meet you." And the two misters shake hands.

Mama says, "Odin went to Wilberforce University for a time. He moved back recently."

I tug on Mr. Coles's coat to tell him the most important information Mama is leaving out. "Mr. Johnson came over and ate supper with us!"

And I'm glad I shared it, too, because I can tell Mr. Coles does not like what I just said.

"I see," Mr. Coles says, and he puts his hat back on his head, and looks away.

Before Mama can share anything else with either mister, Miss Greta butts into the situation, which is not at all what I prayed for.

"Praise the Lord, Odin Johnson has come to church!" Miss Greta says. "So glad to see you! Don't you go anywhere. I have someone I want you to meet!" And Miss Greta is fast-wobbling away.

While our little huddle waits for Miss Greta to return, Mama turns away from Mr. Johnson and turns toward Mr. Coles. What is Mama doing, turning her back on the most handsome bachelor here? I jump between Mr. Coles and Mama, to offer Mr. Coles more information.

"Did you know, Mr. Coles, that Mr. Johnson used to tease my mama when she was my age? I bet you didn't know that! He thought Mama was the prettiest girl in all of Charlottesville. Isn't that right, Mama?"

And then, just then, Mama grabs my hand, bends down, and hard-whispers right in my ear, "What did I tell you? Stitch it."

Mr. Coles puts his hand on Mama's arm. "It's okay, Elizabeth. Really."

Mama stands back up and shakes her head a little. And though Mr. Coles said it was okay, I'm pretty sure I will later be writing one hundred sentences about minding my own business.

Miss Greta comes back over, arm in arm with a young lady wearing a navy-colored dress with a lace collar who's smiling nervously. She looks older than Jocelyn, so I'm guessing she's in her twenties.

Miss Greta plops herself right inside our huddle space and says, "Odin Johnson, I'd like for you to meet my niece, Iris Rucker. And this, Iris, is Raymond Coles. And, of course, you know Elizabeth Lewis and her daughter."

I know from Miss Greta that Iris is a teacher who lives and works in Culpeper, about an hour's drive away, so I have no idea why Miss Greta is introducing her to Mr. Johnson.

"Nice to meet you," Mr. Johnson and Mr. Coles say. Then both misters put their eyes back on Mama, even though Iris is standing right there.

Mr. Johnson finally says to everyone, "Would you all like to walk down to my store? I'd love to show you the chicken-and-dumplings display."

"We've already seen it," Mama says. "Raymond drove me by last night."

And just like that, Mr. Johnson's smile deflates like a tire that has just been punched with a nail.

"Mama!" I say. "Sometimes you are impossible! I haven't seen it yet!"

Everyone ignores me, even Mr. Johnson, which is not at all like him.

"Iris and I would love to walk with you," Miss Greta says. "Wouldn't we, Iris?"

"Yes, Aunt Greta," Iris says, and smiling, she looks right into Mr. Johnson's perfect brown eyes.

So I quick-butt-in. "Miss Greta, you can't go walking to Mr. Johnson's store. What about your knees and your bad back?"

"My knees are fine, honey child," Miss Greta says, and she lifts her leg and shakes it like there's no tomorrow.

And just like that, Miss Greta, Iris, and Mr. Johnson are saying goodbye to Mama, Mr. Coles, and me. They begin walking toward Mr. Johnson's store on West Main Street while Mama, Mr. Coles, and I are walking away from it, even though I've yet to see the display.

What a messed-up Sunday this is turning out to be!

nineteen
WORE-OUT FINGERS

Thankfully, when we get to the corner of Commerce and Third Street NW, Mr. Coles parts ways with us and walks on home. Even after he's gone, Mama doesn't say anything to me about my butting in or about me not minding my own business. The only thing I hear coming from Mama is the sharp sound of her shoes *plap-plap-plapping* on the sidewalk. She's as quiet as a lone gray storm cloud floating above—not a sound of thunder, a flash of lightning, or a gust of wind anywhere. I hope that means she's forgotten about me having to write a hundred sentences if I didn't stich my lips.

But Mama did not forget.

No sooner do we walk into the house than Mama's storm cloud bursts.

And so here I am, stuck in my room writing *I will mind my own business* one hundred times, with Mama cooking dinner without me.

"At least the sentence isn't longer," I say out loud when I'm done with fifty and smell sweet potatoes boiling.

At seventy-five sentences, I smell Mama's green been casserole baking.

When I'm on ninety-five and smell fish frying, I whisper to Mitzy, "It's Mama who should be writing 'I will try harder to understand my daughter' a hundred times. Then maybe she would try harder."

Once my hundred sentences are finished, I stand, stretch my fingers and neck, and try to get the cramps out. I put my now-dull pencils back in their box. Maybe Miss Greta will sharpen them with a paring knife before school starts. I know Mama won't. She'll just say my dull pencils will serve as a reminder about suffering consequences. It could be worse. I could be starting school with nubs for pencils.

I head downstairs and give Mama my one hundred sentences, and am surprised she is sitting at the kitchen table all ready for supper. Has Mama been waiting for me a long time? Is the food ice cold? Why didn't she call me when it was ready? Is she *that* mad at me? Mama doesn't say anything about my sentences being done in the neatest handwriting a person can make, she just stares at the paper without saying a word.

I quick-wash my hands and sit down, hoping my only consequence is writing the sentences and having dull pencils. Nothing more.

Mama says grace. "Lord, thank you for this blessed day, for this food, and please, please, Lord, help my headstrong daughter have some restraint."

What kind of prayer is that! Headstrong daughter? Headstrong daughter! All at once, my inside heat rises so quick I bet it could warm up this ice-cold food.

Without asking to be excused, I get up, not even pushing

in my chair, and storm upstairs. I'm putting myself to bed without taking one bite of Mama's juicy cornmeal-crisp catfish. How can I eat food when Mama asked for the wrong thing? Mama's the one with a headstrong problem!

I crawl into bed without brushing my teeth. I pull the covers over my head without wrapping my scarf around my hair. I pull Mitzy close without changing into my nightgown. And I fall fast asleep without praying for anything. I'm too mad to pray.

When I wake up, I smell sausage cooking, and my mouth waters. But as my thoughts return to what happened last night, I hesitate about going downstairs, even though my empty stomach is grumbling. With it being Labor Day and Mama not having to work, I know she'll be the one downstairs fixing breakfast, not Miss Greta. I'm worried. Will Mama be super angry with me for leaving the supper table in a huff and putting myself to bed without saying good night?

I grab Mitzy, but instead of going downstairs straight away, I head over to my bedroom window and look out to see Mr. Anderson snipping grass around his sidewalk. I see Mr. Charley rocking on his porch chair. I see Miss Viola watering her pots of flowers blooming like fireworks. Seeing the clear blue sky, hearing the chickadees sing, smelling the primroses, watching two squirrels zigzag-chasing—the loveliness of summer's end just outside my window makes me think that breakfast at the kitchen table will be better than supper was last night, and that there's a lot I should be grateful for.

After a while, I hear Mama calling me, because breakfast

is ready. So I head downstairs, hoping Mama and me will start off today better than where we left off yesterday.

"Good morning, sunshine!" she says to me. "I've fixed your favorite—sunny-side up eggs, stewed apples, biscuits, and sausage!"

I run over to Mama, bury myself into her, and start to cry. She kisses the top of my head.

"None of that," she says. "Let's eat!" And we do, until my belly is near to bursting—three biscuits full.

Later that afternoon, whenever I stop practicing my audition piece, I hear the *whir-whir-whirring* of Mama's sewing machine. I believe my coat will be hanging in the closet by morning, ribbon added to the collar and everything.

I decide to take a break from playing my flute to write Jewel another letter, even though I still haven't gotten any replies. Maybe one will come tomorrow.

Dear Jewel,

Today is Labor Day, but we won't be starting school tomorrow because Simon Bowles got polio. His legs are okay. But I'm worried about you. Have kids in Chicago gotten polio, too?

I wish you were here. Then you could help me get my Man-for-Mama Plan back on track. Mama likes Mr. Coles and I'm worried there's not a thing I can do about it.

Will you be playing your saxophone in the band? I want first-chair flute so bad this year, I've been practicing my head off. Maybe Gwen has not been practicing.

Tell Mr. Poindexter I said hello. Please write back soon.

> *Your best, best friend,*
> *Allie*

When I'm finished, I run downstairs to ask Mama for an envelope. She's trimming the seam of what will soon be the sleeve of my new coat.

"I wrote another letter to Jewel. May I have an envelope and three cents for a stamp, please?"

"Great day!" Mama says, like she forgot something. "On my dresser, there's a little envelope from Mrs. McIntire with your name on it. I told her about you missing Jewel and she got you something."

I pop into Mama's room, and carefully open the envelope that has my name written on it in cursive. Inside are ten colorful stamps. Ten! Each has a different national park printed on it. Each is worth a different amount. One stamp is even worth ten cents!

I run back into the living room! "Thank you, Mama!"

"Thank Mrs. McIntire," Mama says, "by making her a little thank-you card."

"I will!" I say, and go upstairs, and do.

twenty
FIRST-DAY BLUES

The first day of school has finally come, and I'm ready. Mama is going to work a little late so she can see me off. She hot-combed my hair, so my bangs are straight with a tad of curl-under. She added a new band of white material from the fabric chest to my dress to make it a little longer and it is now washed, ironed, and clean. My shoes, which still fit, are shined, and my socks are bleached white. Most important, because there's no way I'm starting school with ashy showing, my elbows and knees are Vaseline shiny.

Mama buttons the last button on my sweater and kisses me goodbye. "Behave yourself," she says, sounding as nervous as I feel. "And don't dawdle. You don't have much time before the tardy bell."

"I will," I say to the behave-yourself part. "I won't," I say to the don't-dawdle part, and start walking toward school.

The strap of my satchel, crossing my body, feels familiar, though smaller. It's the same satchel I've used since I started school in first grade. Inside it are my audition music, and my school supplies, which includes my resharpened pencils, thanks to Miss Greta. There's also a glass with my name on it for water, a handkerchief for blowing, and Mitzy for feeling less alone without Jewel. My flute case is too large to fit inside, so I'm carrying it.

It's true what Mama said. I haven't left myself a lot of time before the tardy bell rings, and the teachers at my school are particular about us understanding the importance of being prompt and prepared for the privilege of learning. But knowing Jewel will not be walking with me to school has made me wait until the absolute last minute. I'm hoping to avoid being on the same block at the same time Gwen Turner is headed to school.

When Jewel was beside me, I didn't mind about Gwen Turner and me being in the same time and space. If Gwen ended up walking directly behind Jewel and me, and she was snickering with her best friend, Mary, I didn't care. If Jewel and I ended up walking behind Gwen and Mary, and Gwen seemed to be showing off how bouncy her straightened hair could be, I didn't care. Even if Gwen and Mary ended up walking directly beside us, and Gwen and Mary's conversation would crash into ours, I didn't care. I didn't care because Jewel was beside me saying the right thing to help me with my inside heat. That's why I snuck Mitzy into my satchel today even if I'm not supposed to. If my inside heat tries to get out, I'll peek at Mitzi inside my satchel and imagine she's Jewel.

Of course, Mitzy can't walk beside me, or tell me to calm down, or make me laugh. But she's the best that I can do for the first day of school. I could've walked with Booker T. He came by yesterday and told me I could, but that would just be weird. He's Caesar's friend, not mine. Now, if Booker T. was Caesar, I would definitely walk with him. But at least

Caesar will be waiting for me at the bottom of the school steps, unless he forgot his promise.

I'm thinking fifth grade will be okay even without Jewel so long as Caesar will be not just my same-age cousin, but also my best friend at school. But sometimes Caesar forgets about me, especially when he gets around that wooden-headed Booker T. And so despite Caesar's promises, a worry has burr-stuck itself to me. Without Jewel, will I be able to keep calm if Gwen makes me mad? I hope so!

As I'm passing by Jewel's used-to-be house, I stop to imagine she doesn't live a billion miles away and everything is how I wish it to be.

I'm skipping up to Jewel's door and knocking.

Mr. Poindexter is hollering through the door, "Come in!"

I'm going inside.

Mr. Poindexter is saying, "Morning, Allie. What a lovely brand-new dress you're wearing."

I'm saying, "Shucks, this old thing—I've worn it twice already!"

Then Jewel comes running down the stairs, and the two of us are walking hand in hand on the first day of school.

By the time I look away from Jewel's house, I realize I'm the only kid left on the block! There are no white kids of Charlottesville walking down the sidewalk going one way toward Midway School, and there are no colored kids walking toward Jefferson School, which can mean only one thing. I must be late! And so I start running.

As soon as I turn off Commerce Street, I see Caesar and

Booker T. waiting for me at the bottom of the wide steps leading up to the school. Caesar hasn't forgotten me!

Caesar yells like the school is on fire. "Hurry up, Allie Cat! We're going to be late!"

And we're running up the steps, into the school, toward Mrs. McGinness's classroom, ours for the year, trying to make it before the late bell sounds.

"Decorum, children, enter with decorum," Mrs. McGinness says.

"Yes, ma'am," we say, and slow ourselves down.

"Find your desks," she says.

And then the late bell rings.

"From now on, you'll be seated before the bell rings. Understood?"

"Yes, ma'am," we say again.

I quickly find my desk, the one where Mrs. McGinness has written my name in cursive on a lined piece of paper, and placed it on top of the stack of books that will be mine for the year. I sit down and fold my arms on top of them. I finally feel ready for a new school year to begin.

As Mrs. McGinness reads the roll, and kids are saying "present," I take a quick look around to see where Caesar is seated. He's in the third desk in the first row because his last name is Braxton. I look to see where Booker T.'s desk is. He's five rows down and four rows over because his last name is Thurston. And because Thurston and Turner aren't too far apart in the alphabet, Gwen's desk is next to Booker T.'s, which happens just about every year. Of course, I'm smack-dab in the middle of the classroom of about fifty desks. Sometimes I wish my last name was Anderson instead of Lewis. That way my assigned desk would always be in the front row, and my teacher would call on me whenever my hand was raised. At least my last name isn't Tuvall or something like that, because then my desk, not Booker T.'s, would be next to Gwen's. She'd probably accuse me of cheating whenever I got one hundred on a test! Like I'd need to cheat!

After taking roll, Mrs. McGinness points to a list on the chalkboard that spells out her expectations for the year.

1. *You will take care of your textbooks.*
2. *You will work diligently.*
3. *You will use the ink in your fountain pens sparingly, and only to learn cursive.*
4. *You will use the water glass you brought from home so as not to spread disease.*

"Most importantly," she says, "you will add to the good name of this school by displaying honor, honesty, and courage. You will manifest fine self-respect, maintain a spirit of cooperation, and show thoughtful consideration for others. Is that understood?"

"Yes, ma'am," we all say.

After Mrs. McGinness is finished with her first-day-of-school lecture, we write our names on the inside of our books, right beneath the names of those who have used the books before. I like looking over the list of names to see if I recognize anyone. One time, I got a math book that used to be Jocelyn's. Another time I got a reading book with Mama's maiden name in it! That was amazing! After our books are labeled and all our supplies are "in their proper place," our first day of school learning begins.

"Open your *McGuffey's Fifth Eclectic Reader*," Mrs. McGinness says. "Turn to page thirty-nine." The sound of turning pages fills the classroom. "Who would like to read paragraph one of 'The Good Reader'?"

I quick-raise my hand.

Of course Gwen does, too.

Mrs. McGinness calls on Gwen.

Is this how my fifth grade is going to be? With Gwen being chosen over me—again?

A tongue click against the roof of my mouth escapes. *Nuttt.*

Mrs. McGinness must have heard it, because she shoots a raised eyebrow toward me.

During history, after I've drawn from memory an outline on the chalkboard of the state of Virginia, Mrs. McGinness asks if anyone would like to improve upon it. Not a soul raises their hand except for Gwen!

Gwen sashays up to the board and adds the Virginia Barrier Islands that stick out into the Atlantic like a bumpy apostrophe.

A whispery growl escapes from my chest. *Guhhhh.*

Mrs. McGinness must have heard it, because this time she crosses her arms while shooting a raised eyebrow toward me.

Then, when I incorrectly name the sixth president of the United States as Andrew Jackson, I hear someone giggle. I can't help but turn around, look straight at Gwen, and mouth *Stoppp*, because I'm pretty sure it was her who was giggling.

When I turn back around, Mrs. McGinness is hard-staring right at me—arms still crossed and shaking her head. I don't raise my hand again even when I know the answer to the math equation she writes on the board.

When the bell rings Mrs. McGinness says, "You may be dismissed for lunch. For those of you taking band, take your instruments with you, and head directly to the band room after lunch. Those of you taking choir, go to the room that's next to the band room. After music, join me on the playground for recess."

I grab my flute and satchel and head toward the door with everyone else. But before I leave, Mrs. McGinness stops me.

"Miss Lewis, a word," she says.

Caesar looks back and shakes his head like he's ashamed of me or something. *What did I do?* Gwen was the one making trouble, trying to prove she's smarter than me, better than me at everything—AGAIN.

I stand before Mrs. McGinness's desk. She takes off her glasses and for the longest time just looks at me.

"Ma'am?" I finally ask. "Would you please say something? Because I truly need some nourishment right about now."

"Dear me!" Mrs. McGinness says.

"But it's true," I say. "All I had this morning is oatmeal, and it was a small bowl at that."

"I see I have my work cut out for me!"

"I'll know my presidents next time," I say.

"Miss Lewis..."

"Yes, ma'am," I say, trying my best not to rush her.

"Is the flute a better instrument than a clarinet?"

What on earth is she getting at, I wonder. "I can't play the clarinet," I say.

"Is the flute a better instrument than a clarinet?" she says again, as though the same words said twice will be better understood the second time around.

"I really don't know anything about the clarinet. I play the flute." And I hold up my case to show her. "See."

Mrs. McGinness rubs her temple like she's trying to understand her own question. "Let me ask it this way. What would happen if a flute spent all its time staring at a clarinet, thinking it was a better instrument?"

"I'm sorry, Mrs. McGinness. I just don't follow, and I'm awfully hungry. May I go now?"

Mrs. McGinness's patience is obviously not as thick as Miss Cooper's, my teacher from last year, because Mrs. McGinness says a loud no to my request to get lunch, with such force it makes me blink superfast.

She gets up from her desk and takes a worn, thin green book off the shelf and hands it to me. It's a copy of *Aesop's Fables*. On the cover is a gold tree shaped like a heart with little gold animals all around—a cock, a goose, a frog, a lion, a fox, a mouse, and a big-winged bird. My teacher opens to one of the little stories inside—"The Dog and the Shadow."

"Read it. Illustrate it. And in your own words, tell me the lesson you learn from it," Mrs. McGinness says. "You will have it on my desk by tomorrow morning. Understood?"

"Yes, ma'am...but why? What did I do?"

Without answering my question, she says, "Take care of my little book. It was the second one, right after the Bible, my grandfather bought after the Great Emancipation. I've only loaned it to a few."

"Yes, ma'am," I say, feeling better now, knowing my brand-new teacher has entrusted me with a book her grandfather bought. "I'll take care of it."

"Now go on downstairs for lunch."

Quickly, but carefully, I put Mrs. McGinness's book into my satchel, then hurry myself down to lunch, because I really am famished.

twenty-one
MINDING MANNERS

With so many kids in the cafeteria eating at the same time, the room is warm with bodies and conversations. Miss Cox, our home economics teacher who also fixes us lunch, looks cross when I come in long after everyone else. But of course she feeds me.

When she hands me my bowl of hot vegetable soup, her face seems to ask—*Miss Alexandra Lewis, are you already in hot water, on the first day of school, no less? What a shame.*

Wanting her to think well of me, I wide-smile at her and use my very best manners. "Thank you so much, Miss Cox. It smells delicious."

Miss Cox smiles then, so maybe she's remembering all those times in fourth grade when I wasn't in hot water, and not all those times I was. As I'm searching for a spoon with no water spots, she tells me to hurry along, and so I do. I find Caesar in the crowd, and he's saved a seat for me.

No sooner do I sit down and start eating my soup than Caesar asks, "Did you get a paddling?"

"Do I look like I've been crying?" I take another slurp.

"Why were you throwing those angry looks at Gwen?" Booker T. asks.

I point my spoon at him. "None of your beeswax."

"Sorry!" Booker T. says, then he gets up to place his bowl on the table where the dirty dishes go.

Worried I won't have time to finish my soup, I lift up my bowl and start slurping.

"Don't let Miss Cox catch you eating like that," Caesar says while standing up. "Or you'll end up practicing table manners after school!"

But I'm not worried about Miss Cox catching me not minding my manners because I've already finished my soup, and just in time, too. The bell rings and it's time for band!

All at once, I feel my heart jitterbug-dancing. Audition time!

I grab my satchel and flute case, and think about running to the band room, but when I see a third-grade teacher standing in the hallway thwacking his hand with a wooden ruler, I slow myself down, and walk with decorum beside Caesar and Booker T.

"Have you been practicing your audition music?" Caesar asks me.

"Why do you even have to ask! Of course I've been practicing! I want first chair. You know that."

Booker T., being the naysayer that he is, says, "Gwen is an amazing flute player. She'll probably get first chair."

I give Booker's arm a bop with my fist.

"*Ow!*" he says, rubbing his arm. "What you do that for?"

"You know full well why!" I say. "Besides, it didn't hurt."

"It hurt, all right," he says, smiling ear to ear. "You throw a mean right hook... for a girl." Then he pretend-boxes the air.

"Even if Gwen gets first chair this year," Caesar says to me, "that doesn't mean you're not a great flute player, too."

So I bop Caesar's arm.

"*Ow!*" Caesar says. "What's that for?"

"For saying what you just said!"

When I walk into the band room, I try very hard NOT to remember how Mr. Coles looked when he came to take my mama dancing. I try to see only Mr. Coles my band teacher standing there at his conductor stand.

"Find your instrument section, and have a seat in any chair," Mr. Coles says.

As he says it, Caesar and Booker T. go to the percussion section. I sit with the other flute players, but nowhere near Gwen.

"Welcome to fourth- and fifth-grade band!" he says. "Ready for a great year?"

"Ready," we all say.

As usual, the first thing Mr. Coles does is have us tune our instruments. He hits a little triangle. It plays a C. And when we play the same note, we listen. If the note coming from our instrument is a tad bit higher or sharper than the triangle's C or a tad bit lower or flatter, then we adjust our instruments. Tuning is kind of fun. I like knowing how to move the head joint of my flute in or out to the perfect spot until my C blends with the sounds of all the other instruments, like we're playing on the same radio frequency, with no sound static coming from anyone.

The second thing we do is play our warm-up scales. I try to hear Gwen's flute among the others, to see how good her tone is. But I can't hear the sound of one flute over another since everyone is playing like they've really missed being in band.

"That was copacetic!" Mr. Coles says. "Just great! Now it's time for you to audition for your assigned seat. Hopefully, everyone has practiced these past two weeks. That said, don't get discouraged if you don't play as well as you'd like, because this year I've decided to have tryouts for your seat placements every nine weeks. Anyone can be moved up if they practice, practice, practice. And anyone can be moved down if they stop practicing."

Mr. Coles's new rule doesn't have me worried. I know I'll be practicing all year. If I get first chair, no one will be able to bump me down to second.

When it's time for the flutes to audition, I keep blowing a steady flow of air into mine to keep it warm, in tune, and ready to play. Out of the seven kids who will be playing flute this year, three are in fourth grade and four are in fifth. As each one plays, my hope at getting first chair grows. Finally, only Gwen and I have yet to try out.

"Miss Turner," Mr. Coles says, "come on up."

Gwen walks up to Mr. Coles's conductor stand and puts her audition music on it. I feel my nose scrunching at her oh-so-perfect-posture. When she places her flute to her lips to play, I hold my breath. Her notes come flowing out clear and sharp, warm and bright, sweet and sure. Her audition is perfect.

"Excellent," Mr. Coles proud-says. Then he calls my name. "Miss Lewis."

I walk up, stand in front of the music stand, and look out. Everyone is staring at me, wondering, doubting. Who will play the best? Allie or Gwen? And deep down, I'm thinking I don't have a chance. But I pull my flute up to my lips and let the notes fly anyway.

When the final measure of my audition is done, the quiet of the room pulls at the muscles in my neck and shoulders and up into my ears. *Did I at least play okay*, I wonder.

Then, all at once, everyone is clapping (everyone except Gwen), and Caesar is proud-pointing his drumsticks at me, saying, "That's my cousin! Don't you forget it."

Mr. Coles kind-smiles at me. "Well," he says. "That was some fine flute playing—very fine indeed." And he writes my name in his book. "Miss Lewis, you'll be in first chair. Miss Turner, you'll be in second—"

"Uncle Raymond!" Gwen practically shouts, but he just ignores her and keeps assigning chairs.

I really can't believe it. I'll be seated in first chair, while Gwen will be in second! I'll be playing the flute solos, while Gwen will be listening! I'll be leading the songs, while Gwen will be following. And I'm going to practice, practice, practice so I stay seated in the first chair all year long. This feeling of being first feels so fine I'd like to can it and save it forever and a day! And though I still think Mr. Coles is wrong for Mama, he sure is all right as a band teacher.

twenty-two
TSK!

Once we leave band and head outside for recess, Caesar says to me, "Congratulations! You got first chair!"

"Of course I did," I say. "I practiced and practiced until I was better than Gwen."

"You don't have to be so smug about it," Caesar says.

"I'm not being smug, just proud, that's all."

"Try being proud without comparing yourself to Gwen, then maybe you wouldn't sound so smug," Caesar says. "Besides, she looked fuming mad when her uncle gave you first chair."

"Do I look worried?" I say.

"You should be." Caesar pretend-bites his nails.

"Well, I'm not."

Booker T. comes running over. "Come on, Caesar. We need a pitcher."

"Booker T., what did you think of my audition?" I ask.

"You did all right," Booker T. says like he wasn't just there to hear how well I played. "Want to play ball with us?"

"Not today," I say. "I want to look at a book Mrs. McGinness gave me."

After Caesar and Booker T. join some other kids to play

baseball with a stick bat and a ball of rolled-up rubber bands, I go over to a tree stump that makes for a perfect place to sit. When I open my satchel, I see Mitzy looking at me. I smile at her, but I don't take her out. Just as I'm reaching for Mrs. McGinness's book of fables, I hear Gwen Turner's voice right behind me. I turn to face her and she's looking straight into my satchel, staring down at Mitzy. And what does Gwen do? She grabs my doll!

I jump up and yell, "Give her back, Gwen!"

But Gwen spins away from me and starts loud-singing for everyone to hear! *"Look who's got a baby doll! A baby doll! A baby doll! Look who's got a baby doll. It's Allie Cat!"*

"Give her back!" I yell again.

Gwen takes off running with Mitzy in her paws! All the while she's singing. *"Look who's got a baby doll! A baby doll! A baby doll! Look who's got a baby doll. It's Allie Cat!"*

I run after her, my inside heat boiling over.

"Look who's got a baby doll! A baby doll! A baby doll! Look who's got a baby doll. It's Allie Cat!"

"Give her back! She's *mi-nnnnne!*" I say, right on Gwen's heels.

And then I catch up to that Gwen Turner. I tackle her to the ground. I straddle her. I hard-hit her. She hard-hits me. She pulls my hair. I pull hers. She tries to push me off. I keep her on the ground, because nobody—NOBODY—messes with Mitzy!

While I'm fighting, I see Caesar over me, begging me to stop. I see Booker T. over Gwen, begging her to stop. But it's Mrs. McGinness who is upon us now, making the tumbling stop. She grabs hold of Gwen's arm with one hand. She grabs hold of mine with the other. She pulls us up from the dirt.

And where's Mitzy?

She's lying nearby, looking up at me with great big disappointed eyes.

"What do you have to say for yourselves?" Mrs. McGinness shouts, though I know full well she doesn't want an answer. "Is this how young ladies act? I never!"

"My doll!" I out-of-breath say, trying to reach for Mitzy. But my teacher just takes Gwen and me by the wrists straight to the office.

Thankfully, out of the corner of my eye, I see Caesar rescuing Mitzy from the ground. Of course there's no one to rescue me from the heap of trouble I know I'm in.

Mrs. McGinness commands us to sit down on the chairs inside the office, then goes into the principal's office. I slip my hands under my legs and bite my lip. I can hear Mrs. McGinness talking to Mr. Duncan, which makes me bite my lip harder. I think the school secretary, Miss Perkins, can hear them, too, because she looks over at us, which makes me look away.

There's a chair between Gwen and me, and I'm glad, because I still want to hit her, though not as hard.

I hear Gwen sniffling. *Who's the B-A-B-Y now?* I want to say out loud, but of course I don't say anything, because Miss Perkins is right there.

Pretty soon, Mrs. McGinness comes out of Mr. Duncan's office, but before she goes back to our classroom she stops and *long-squints* at us above the rims of her glasses. And though there are no words coming out of her mouth, I know what her eyes are saying—*tsk-tsk-tsk*—which makes me think maybe I should've just tackled Gwen to get Mitzy back, without any hitting.

As I wait to go in to see the principal, the sound of Miss Perkins's typewriter keys striking paper says *tsk-tsk-tsk* over and over, which makes me think maybe I should've just pushed Gwen, without any tackling.

When Caesar comes into the office carrying my books, flute, and satchel (with a dirty Mitzy peeking out), the sound of his shoes *tsk-tsk-tsks* across the floor, which makes me think maybe I should've just yelled at Gwen to get Mitzy back, without any pushing.

After Caesar leaves, and Booker T. comes in with Gwen's books, flute, and satchel, he clears his throat—*tsk-tsk-tsk*—and I know.

I should not have hit.

I should not have tackled.

I should not have pushed.

I should not have been fighting like a fool.

Why, oh, why didn't I calm myself down?

Why didn't I keep control over my inside heat?

Why didn't I get Mitzy back some other way?

Surely, Caesar would've helped me. Gwen really likes Caesar.

All at once, I'm-truly-sorry tears start trying their best to creep out, but I'm keeping them sucked in.

Mr. Duncan opens his door right then and tells Gwen and me to bring our things and come inside. He shuts the door behind us, and tells us to sit down. His bass-drum voice is booming. He looks at me. He looks at Gwen. He looks down on his desk at two envelopes that I'm sure have yellow discipline sheets inside them. Then he looks back at us. All the while he's looking, he's rapping his pencil on his desk, which makes me feel the need to run and use the restroom.

Finally, Mr. Duncan stops rapping his pencil. "Do you two young ladies realize the seriousness of what has happened?" he asks.

"Yes, sir," Gwen and I both say.

"What do you have to say for yourself, Miss Turner?"

"I'm sorry," she says, though she can't quite look at me when she says it.

"Miss Lewis?"

"I'm sorry," I say to Gwen, though I can't quite look at her when I say it.

"You should be sorry!" Mr. Duncan slaps his pencil on the desk. I'm surprised it doesn't break. "You both know that we absolutely do not tolerate fighting in this school! And it will not happen again! Understand?"

"Yes, sir," we say again.

He stands up and hands us each an envelope from his desk. "Have your parents read and sign these. Return them to me tomorrow."

"Yes, sir," we say again.

Mr. Coles comes in then. Is he here because Gwen is like his daughter? Have I made him so upset that he's come to tell me he's taking first chair away from me?

"Here you go," Mr. Coles says in an I'm-disappointed

voice. And he hands Mr. Duncan some music. "I would like for them to practice this duet for their work here with you. They'll be playing it for the concert." Then he leaves.

Mr. Duncan says, "For the rest of the week, you will report to my office every morning to work on your lessons. Miss Lewis, you will sit there." He points to the desk facing the wall on the right of his office. "And Miss Turner, there." He points to the desk on the other side. "Mrs. McGinness and Miss Cox will be dropping off your assignments, as Mr. Coles just did. I'm going to ask Miss Perkins to listen to you practice your duet during my lunch break. You will dot every *i* and cross every *t* of each assignment. And I will send a letter at the end of each day letting your parents know how you behaved. Have I made myself perfectly clear?"

"Yes, sir," we say again.

"One more thing. Miss Lewis, unless it's show-and-tell you are not to bring toys to school."

And though I want to say that Mitzy's not a toy, she's my should-be-Jewel friend, I only say, "Yes, sir."

"Here is your music to take home so you can start practicing. Once you put your books on your desks you can leave. I'm dismissing you a little early so you can use the extra time to think about your actions today."

I take my time as I walk home, wanting to get there at the usual time so Miss Greta won't notice that I was dismissed from school early like in-trouble kids. While I'm slow-walking home, it seems the whole world knows it was me who made a poor choice at school today. The Minors' hound dog howls—*Who's in trouble? You!* Mrs. Carver's baby cries—*Who's in trouble? You!* Mr. Tonsler's tools clang *Who's in trouble? You?* And of course I know it's true. I've managed to get myself into a heap of trouble on the first day of fifth grade, just when it was going so well. And all that's left for me to do is silent-pray, all the way home, *Please, oh please, don't let Mama change her mind about never using a switch on me.*

No sooner do I get home than I run upstairs, without telling Miss Greta a thing.

I pull Mitzy out of my satchel to look her over. Her dress is dirty. Her face is dirty. And her hair is a mess! I quick-take-off her dress, and run downstairs to wash it. Miss Greta sees me filling up the washtub and taking out the washboard.

"What happened to Mitzy's dress?" she asks.

"Nothing," I say, trying not to cry.

"Did you take your doll to school?"

"I won't anymore," I say.

Thankfully, Miss Greta asks me no more questions, so I start washing Mitzy's dress. Once it's clean, I run outside to clothespin it on the line. Tony, a neighborhood boy who plays marbles with his friends in the alley near our house, sees me and comes running over.

"Hey," he says.

"Hay is for horses," I say, which means *leave me alone.*

"I bet you're gonna get it when your mama gets home," Tony says.

"Go away, Tony!" I yell, then run back into the house.

When I get inside, I hear Miss Greta talking to Mrs.

Goins from three blocks over! How fast her feet must have carried her over here—all so she could be the first to tell Miss Greta about my business. Too bad Mrs. Goins's mother never made her write *I will mind my own business* a hundred times! I scooch through the kitchen and climb up the stairs in a hurry to clean Mitzy's face and fix her hair before I have to face Miss Greta. But no sooner do I take Mitzy into the bathroom than I hear Miss Greta coming. I quick-run into my room and jump into bed—clothes and shoes and all—and cover my head like I'm sleeping. Maybe Miss Greta will think I'm napping. But I'm wrong!

Miss Greta pulls back my covers and stands over me—hands on her hips like she's an army commander with red-hot-poker eyes. "Sit up!" she says. "Why did I have to find out what happened from a neighbor? You should have told me yourself!"

"I'm sorry."

"Lord have mercy! Hasn't your mama had enough grief in her life!" Miss Greta says. "Do you want to cause her more?"

I shake my head, because that's the last thing I'd ever want. I want to make my mama's life easier, not harder. That's why I want her to marry Mr. Johnson.

"Child, don't you know there's a moment in time between thinking and feeling and saying and doing? You got to grab hold of that space by making better choices. Are you listening to me?"

"I'm listening, Miss Greta."

"I hope so! Because your mama's not raising a fool! Now where's the envelope I know Mr. Duncan sent home?"

I get up from my bed, reach into my satchel, and give it to Miss Greta.

"I'll be handing this to your mama the second she gets home. And you are not to leave this room until then."

"But Miss Greta, Mitzy's in the bathroom. I was just about to clean her."

"She'll just have to stay dirty, because you're staying in this room. Have I made myself perfectly clear?"

"But—"

"No buts." Miss Greta slams my door behind her.

Sitting on the edge of my bed, I think about Mitzy, lying all dirty in the bathroom sink, and then I think on what Miss Greta said. Was there a moment of time between when I felt like hitting Gwen and when I hit her? It sure didn't seem like there was.

After remaking my bed, I take out Mrs. McGinness's book, *Aesop's Fables*, and begin reading "The Dog and His Shadow." I want to do a good job on my assignment. Maybe Mrs. McGinness will see my report and think, *Miss Lewis is all right in my book, maybe she was having an off day yesterday.*

It only takes minutes to read the story, seeing how it's just a few lines long. When I'm done, I scratch my head, trying to think of the lesson the story is supposed to be teaching. Nothing comes to me, so I draw a picture of the story first.

I fold my paper so it has four even sections. In the first section, I draw a pool of water. In the second, I draw a dog with a chunk of meat in his mouth, staring into the pool. In the third, I draw the dog snarling at his reflection in the pool, and the reflection snarling back. On the fourth, I draw the meat falling out of the dog's mouth and splashing into the pool of water. When I've drawn in every little detail I can think of, the only lesson that comes to me is "Only a fool dog loses what it's got, because of wanting what its reflection has," which is kind of a strange lesson, if you ask me, because anyone with half a brain knows it's foolish to be jealous of your own reflection.

After drawing and writing my sentence, I decide to read more of *Aesop's Fables*. I like how short they are, and I like the pictures that go with them. While I'm reading, I almost forget about the trouble I'm in—until Mama gets home.

I hear Mama come in. Then, I hear Miss Greta telling her what happened. Next, I hear Mama *thump-thump-thump* up the stairs toward the bathroom, then *stomp-stomp-stomp* toward me. I'm holding my breath when she storms through my bedroom door.

Mr. Duncan's discipline sheet trembles in one of Mama's hands. Mitzy shakes in the other. "My daughter was fighting?" she yells.

I try to explain. "Gwen—Gwen—she snatched Mitzy—she—she wouldn't—"

"Stop it right now! Stop making excuses!"

"But Mama, don't you want to know what happened?"

"I know what happened!" Mama says, then she holds up Mitzy like it's her fault I was fighting.

I bite my lip, but start crying anyway. "I'm—I'm—I'm real sorry, Mama. I was wrong. I shouldn't have hit Gwen, even if she did snatch Mitzy from my bag."

"I've had it with you and this doll!" Mama yells.

I run toward Mama, hoping to stop her from doing what I fear she might do. I hear my voice cracking. "Mama, you're not going to throw her away, are you?"

"If this doll is more important to you than you doing the right thing, more important than controlling your temper, more important than staying in school and getting your education then yes, maybe I will throw her away!"

"Oh, Mama...," I say, tears streaming this way and that, "please, please don't throw Mitzy away. She means so much to me."

"But you," Mama says, her voice a little softer now, "you mean more!"

Then, just then, an unexpected thing happens. Mama grabs hold of me the way I grab Mitzy at night. She tight-hugs me, and starts hard-crying, which of course make me hard-cry, too.

Hearing Mama's tears come tumbling, rumbling, grumbling from deep inside her makes me feel worse than if Mr. Duncan had given me a paddling.

"Allie," Mama finally says after her tears trickle, then drip, then stop. "Learn this now, while you're young. If you jump, the floor will shake. If you throw, the thing will fall. If you fight, there will be consequences, even if you're sorry."

"I understand," I say.

"I don't think so," Mama says, looking at me through puffy eyes.

"Please, Mama," I say as she heads toward the door with

Mitzy. "Don't let Mitzy be my consequence. Don't throw her away."

"I'm not throwing her away." Mama's voice is stronger now. "But I am placing her on top of the icebox, and there she'll stay until I get word from Mr. Duncan that you have behaved yourself in his office the rest of this week, that you've gotten along with Gwen, and that you've played the duet to the best of your ability. Understood?"

"Yes, ma'am."

"You can start practicing now."

twenty-three
TRYING HARDER

When Mama leaves, I pull out the music and study the duet Gwen and I will be playing for the concert. It's "Allegro for a Musical Clock" no. 3, composed by Ludwig van Beethoven. The duet is in the key of G major, so it has only one sharp—F-sharp. That will be easy to remember. But the song has a bunch of sixteenth notes, and that will be hard to play. There are also a lot of places between measures where I'll be needing a deep breath, and at one point toward the end, I'll have to hold my breath and trill like a little bird for seven measures. What has Mr. Coles done, giving me a duet this hard to learn? What if I mess up at the concert? Then everyone along with Gwen will be laughing at me!

I open my flute case, put my flute together, and try playing my part. At first, I can barely get my fingers to cooperate. But soon they begin to understand the note changes. After a while, the notes start turning themselves into a we're-getting-along song and I can see why Mr. Coles has chosen it. It's easy to imagine how nice this music will sound as a duet; at least, if Gwen is practicing her part, too.

* * *

The next morning at breakfast I refuse to look up at Mitzy. Even as I swirl a dab of butter and a spoon of sugar into my Malt-O-Meal, I'm not looking. Even as I smear persimmon jam on my toast, I'm not looking. Even while Miss Greta fusses at me for acting like a child with no sense yesterday, I'm not looking. But when I have to put the orange juice into the icebox, I can't help but see her—dirty, no dress, mussed up hair, and all alone.

"I won't grieve Mama by my actions today, Miss Greta," I say. "I promise, but I'll be the one grieving if Mitzy stays all dirty and undressed on top of the icebox where I have to see her!"

Miss Greta looks up at Mitzy. "I'll take care of it."

"Thank you, Miss Greta!" I say. "And if you don't mind, could you iron her dress, maybe add a little starch?" She *harumphs* like she minds, so I soften my demands by adding, "I'd truly appreciate it."

"I said I'd take care of it. Now go on with your sassy self. You don't want to be late."

"Yes, ma'am," I say, then I give her a big old I'm-grateful-for-your-ironing-with-starch hug.

I place the envelope with the sheet Mama signed for Mr. Duncan in my satchel along with my assignment for Mrs. McGinness. I button up my sweater, grab my satchel and flute, and open the back door to leave. What a surprise! Mr. Johnson is at the back door about to walk in, just like he's family!

"Mr. Johnson!" I say, hoping he doesn't notice Mitzy on the icebox. "Good morning!"

"Good morning, Allie, Miss Greta!" he says, wide-smiling.

His face is as cheery as blue skies after days of thick clouds, so I'm thinking he hasn't heard about yesterday.

"Glad I caught you before you left for school," he says. "Wanted you and Miss Greta to know we've sold out of chicken and dumplings, and I'm putting in another order. Do you think you can make twenty-four jars before the weekend?"

I look at Miss Greta and wonder: Will she say I can't make more this time because of being in trouble? Or will she help me with canning after school this week? After all, seeing how I have to complete all my schoolwork while I'm in Mr. Duncan's office, I won't have homework, other than practicing my duet.

Miss Greta says, "Yes we can! So long as it's okay with Lizzie," which makes me even more grateful for Miss Greta. After all, the more chicken and dumplings we can make for Mr. Johnson to sell, the more chances there are for Mr. Johnson to have a reason to be at our house and find Mama home. And the more Mama visits with Mr. Johnson, the less chance there is for her to visit with Mr. Coles.

"Great!" says Mr. Johnson. "I'll stop by tomorrow morning to see if it's okay, and if it is, I'll bring the supplies over after I close up shop." Then I notice him noticing Mitzy.

"Nice to see you, Mr. Johnson," I say, "but I've really got to go. And don't worry yourself about Mitzy. She will be right as rain by this afternoon. Isn't that right, Miss Greta?"

"Alexandra Lewis, go on to school!" Miss Greta says.

When I'm about halfway to school, Booker T. comes running up to me. "Can I walk with you?"

"I can't stop you," I say like it doesn't much matter, though deep down I'm happy he asked. Walking alone, especially when you know you're headed to the principal's office, is no fun at all.

"Did you get a whupping last night?" he asks.

"My mama doesn't believe in using a switch."

"Oh," he says. "That's nice. Too bad my dad feels otherwise." He rubs his backside, then says "YOW!" like he's a character from a comic strip.

His antics make me laugh, because I know his dad wouldn't put a real hurting on him.

"Do you have to clean the chalkboards after school? Or sit in the dunce chair all day? Or write two hundred fifty sentences? What's your punishment?"

"I have to take my lessons with Gwen in Mr. Duncan's office... for the rest of the week!"

"Oh, man, I think I'd prefer a whupping."

"And worse, Mama says I can't have my doll back until she's gotten word from Mr. Duncan that Gwen and I have played our duet together perfectly, and the duet is really hard."

"Perfectly? Two whuppings would be easier."

"Well, maybe she didn't say 'perfectly.' But still!" I'm very surprised Booker T. understands how I feel.

The rest of the way to school, Booker T. tells me all about

the latest adventure of *Flash Gordon*, which I actually find interesting. When we get to school, Caesar is waiting.

"Hey, cuz!" he says. "Did you get a whupping?"

Booker T. answers for me. "Nope. It's worse."

I nod my head in agreement, then after giving Caesar a quick hug, I reach into my satchel for Mrs. McGinness's book and my drawing of "The Dog and His Shadow," which I had folded neatly and placed inside the book.

"Will you give this to Mrs. McGinness for me?" I ask Caesar, but both he and Booker T. are replying "Sure" at the exact time, which makes me smile.

Of course, I hand the book to Caesar.

"So... you won't be in class?" Caesar asks.

Booker T. answers for me again. "Nope. She's got to spend the rest of the week doing her classwork in the principal's office—with Gwen!"

"Wow. That's bad. Well, I guess you'll never throw a fist again."

"Never," I say.

When I enter the main office and Miss Perkins smiles at me, I think that maybe going to the principal's office for the rest of the week won't be as bad as I'm thinking it will be.

"Go on in," Miss Perkins says. "He's expecting you."

"Good morning," Mr. Duncan says. "You have something for me?"

"Yes, sir," I say, and I hand Mr. Duncan the envelope Mama gave me to give to him.

I watch him open it up and take out the discipline sheet Mama has signed, and her letter to him. A sideways smile spreads across his face as he's reading Mama's note, which makes me wonder what on earth she wrote.

When he's done reading, he says to me, "Don't just stand there, take a seat."

I sit down at the desk that is to be mine for the next four school days. It's piled high with my work for the day. I sit my flute case and satchel down next to the desk. Pretty soon, Gwen comes in. She hands Mr. Duncan her parents' envelope, then has a seat at her desk, also piled high with work. She puts her flute case and satchel down next to it.

After the Pledge of Allegiance, Mr. Duncan tells us that every assignment must be completed with our utmost diligence, and if not, our troubles will only be compounded.

When I'm done reading my assigned pages in my literature book, I write a summary of the story I read. It's about a little girl named Ernestine and a king. When I'm done reading about John Mercer Langston, a colored man from Louisa County who served as a U.S. Congressman from Virginia during Reconstruction, I write a paragraph about him and draw a picture of him looking fine in his suit and bow tie. When I'm done reading my assigned pages in my math book, I do twenty double-digit multiplication figures.

I imagine how different this day would be if I was stuck in Mr. Duncan's office with Jewel instead of Gwen. Not that Jewel and I would ever have ended up in here, unless maybe for bringing toads to school. If I were stuck in here with Jewel, it would almost be fun! I can see us now, turning around to make silly faces at each other, or passing notes with hilarious pictures whenever Mr. Duncan wasn't looking.

But of course it's not Jewel I'm stuck in Mr. Duncan's office with.

I jump a little when Miss Perkins comes in. "Tidy up your desks," she says. "It's time for lunch, and bring your flutes. We'll be practicing your duet after you've eaten."

After we've pushed in our chairs and are about to leave, Mr. Duncan says, "Give Miss Perkins something good to report."

"Yes, sir," Gwen and I say, and we follow Miss Perkins out of Mr. Duncan's office to a small table behind her desk that already has our lunch trays on it.

Miss Perkins points to where we should sit, which means Gwen and I will be facing each other all during lunch.

twenty-four
FACING EACH OTHER FOR THE SAKE OF THE MUSIC

I find myself trying my best not to look directly at Gwen even if we're facing each other. Even if we're facing each other while we're both putting napkins on our laps. Even if we're facing each other while slurping delicious soup with lentils. I may be facing Gwen, but I refuse to place my eyeballs directly on hers!

After I'm done eating, I look up at the ceiling and use multiplication to count the number of tiles. While I'm counting rows of tiles going down, then across, I hear Gwen humming "A Little Night Music."

Ever since learning that song for our fall concert last year, it's been one of my favorites, but I refuse to hum along with Gwen, even though I want to. Soon, though, instead of counting tiles by sevens, my fingers are keeping time to Gwen's humming, moving up and down on the table in front of me. I catch Gwen noticing my fingers, which makes my cheeks get warm.

"Lunchtime is over," Miss Perkins finally says. "Let's take

a bathroom break before you begin practicing your duet. Leave your trays and bring your flutes and music."

I button up my sweater. Gwen buttons up hers. I pick up my music and flute case. Gwen picks up hers. And both of us follow Miss Perkins. At first, Gwen and I are walking side by side, but then she walks faster, so she's beside Miss Perkins and I'm behind. I walk faster to catch up. No one is leaving me behind! Once we're at the bathroom, Miss Perkins stands outside in the hallway while Gwen and I go in. No sooner do we get inside than Gwen faces me—eyeball to eyeball.

"This is your fault, Alexandra Lewis! Don't you forget it! And you better keep your mama away from my uncle! You hear me!" And Gwen pokes me!

I really can't believe it! I stare at the place on my arm where Gwen just poked me. And though I feel my teeth clenching, my hand on my flute grasping, and my lips pressing, I seize the moment between feeling and doing, and don't poke Gwen back. Instead, I stand a little closer to her, and without laying a hand on her, I give Gwen a piece of my mind. "Who do you think *you* are telling *me* to keep *my* mama from *your*—"

Miss Perkins must hear us, because she steps inside.

"Silence! Get your business done now!" she says. And she stands inside the bathroom, leaving unspoken words tussling inside me, wishing for an escape. *You better keep your mama away from my uncle? Like my mama's not good enough for her uncle! If my mama wants to go dancing with her uncle, she* will *go dancing! I'm not keeping my mama from her uncle just because she says so! Who does Gwen think she is? Just* because her family's got a car and a nice house, doesn't mean my mama's not good enough for her uncle! *You better keep your mama away from my uncle?* Ha!

After we use the bathroom, I decide to walk with Miss Perkins on the side where Gwen is not walking, because I don't want my inside heat to rise higher than it's already risen. But once we're in our little library, I realize I will have to stand next to Gwen to practice the duet because Miss Perkins has the music stands set up side by side, almost touching. I grab one of the stands, and move it as far away from Gwen's as I can, which is not at all far enough.

"It's better when playing a duet," Miss Perkins says, "if you play next to each other."

Of course Miss Perkins knows about music. She plays the church organ like nobody's business. But she has no idea how dangerous it is for my inside heat to be any closer to Gwen than where I am right now! I take a deep breath and try to once again seize the moment like Miss Greta said and calm myself down, but I do not move the stand.

"It's not a suggestion," Miss Perkins says to me. "Move your stand back where I had it."

So even though I don't want to, I move my stand back, place my music on it, and focus not on Gwen's words or poke, but on playing the duet so I can get out of trouble with Mama and get Mitzy back.

"You may start on the count of three," Miss Perkins says, setting the tempo, slow and steady. "One-and-two-and-three."

After we're done, Miss Perkins says, "That was totally unacceptable. I know you girls realize the seriousness of playing this duet, and playing it well. Remember, Mr. Duncan will be letting your parents know how you do today. Let's try again." And we do.

Miss Perkins sighs when we're done. She says, "Professional musicians listen to each other or the music won't sync up properly. I know you know this!"

This time when we play, I tap my foot to Miss Perkins's tempo. Gwen must be tapping, too, because it does sound better.

"Much improved," Miss Perkins says. Then she asks us what we think.

"She was playing too slow," I say, frowning at Gwen.

"She was playing too fast," Gwen says, frowning back at me. "If I was playing the melody, I bet it would sound better!"

"I don't know about that!" I say, shaking my head.

"Enough," Miss Perkins says. "Play it one more time, but this time face each other. Listen to one another. Be one flute, not two."

This time, I try my best to ignore Gwen while at the same time paying attention to the sound of her flute. We're still not starting each measure exactly together, so I quick-peek over my music stand to see if Gwen is concentrating, but when I do, I lose my place. It takes me an entire measure before I can come back in.

"Let's hope you'll try harder tomorrow," Miss Perkins says when we're done practicing for the day. "And try smiling at each other. An audience can tell, just from the sound, if a person is frowning while playing."

When we get back to Mr. Duncan's office, he's in the

middle of wiping his mouth with a cloth napkin. He leans back in his chair and asks Miss Perkins how we did.

Thankfully, Miss Perkins doesn't mention the sharp words in the bathroom or the playing while frowning. She just says, "Tomorrow they'll do better," which is not quite the same as saying "They did their best."

After Miss Perkins leaves, Mr. Duncan tells us to have a seat and get started on our home economics project. I take out the needle, thread, and scrap of material Miss Cox sent for us as work and get started on a running stitch, which she expects to be as straight as a paper's edge. As I move the needle up and down through the cloth, my inside heat over Gwen's words, her poke, and her bad flute-playing begins to melt away. When I'm finished, I run my hand over the stitches. My work is as smooth as dumpling dough. Miss Cox will approve. I look over at Gwen and she's done, too.

"For the last hour of school," Mr. Duncan says, "I want you to interview one another." He hands each of us a sheet of paper and a list of questions. I hard-swallow when I see the questions.

1. *Why do you like playing the flute?*
2. *What is your favorite subject in school and why?*
3. *What is your favorite season and why?*
4. *What would you like to do when you grow up?*
5. *What do you do well outside of school?*
6. *Describe a challenge you recently overcame.*
7. *When have you ever felt scared?*
8. *What is your favorite memory?*

9. *What do you love about your family and your community?*
10. *What qualities do you feel make for a good friend?*

"You will write each other's replies down. Afterward, you will use your notes to write a biographical sketch about the other. I'll be grading you, forty points out of forty. Nothing less than thirty-five points will be accepted. You will receive ten points for the overall composition, ten for penmanship, ten for spelling, and ten for the overall tone, which must be positive. In other words, I want you to extol the fine attributes of one another."

Extol the fine attributes—of Gwen? That's a joke!

"*Ummmm—uhhhhh—*" Gwen is stammering. "What does 'extol' mean?"

Mr. Duncan clears his throat, stands up, gets a dictionary off the shelf, and hands it to me.

"I know what 'extol' means," I say. "Why should I look it up?"

"Because I handed you the dictionary," he says.

I find the definition and read it aloud. "Extol: Latin *extollere*, to lift up, to praise highly."

Gwen bursts out laughing. "You want me to extol HER?"

Mr. Duncan gets angry then, and I'm glad it was Gwen who said it and not me—even though I was thinking it, too.

"Have you young ladies learned nothing?" Mr. Duncan's voice booms as he takes the dictionary from me and plops it on his desk. *Boom!*

"Well!" he says. "What are you waiting for? Move your desks

and chairs so they are beside one another, and Miss Lewis, you begin by interviewing Miss Turner."

I move my chair and desk to be beside Gwen's. I sit back down and pick up my dull pencil, not at all ready to ask Gwen Mr. Duncan's fool questions, much less write down her replies. *Extol her fine attributes?* Ha! At least she'll have to extol mine!

Mr. Duncan clears his throat, and I begin interviewing Gwen. Slowly Gwen answers Mr. Duncan's questions. Slowly I write her replies. It's not going as bad as I thought it would, especially since her answers are short and sweet. But when I get to question number seven "When have you ever felt scared?" Gwen jumps up from her chair, startling both Mr. Duncan and me.

She bursts out, "I'm not answering that! No way!"

"Sit down," Mr. Duncan says, "and answer the question."

Gwen does not sit down. "I refuse to tell *her* what scares me. She'll use it against me to make fun of me. I know she will!"

I jump up. "I've never made fun of her! She's the one always making fun of me!"

"That's not true!" Gwen yells, even though we're standing right in front of the principal.

"Yes, it is," I say. "What about that time I was learning to read and you laughed at me?"

"I didn't laugh!"

"Yes, you did!"

"*Nuh-uh*! What about the time I couldn't remember my

line during our third-grade play?" she says. "You laughed at me in front of everybody!"

"I didn't laugh!" I say, which isn't exactly true.

"Yes, you did!"

Finally, Mr. Duncan jumps in, but this time his voice is calm and low. "Girls, have a seat." And so we do.

I feel my heart *beat-beat-beating*, the same as if I'd been jumping rope. I can't believe Gwen remembers the one time I laughed at her! The only time she did something less than perfect.

Mr. Duncan leans forward on his desk. "How about the two of you wipe the slate clean, starting today. Use my interview questions to get to know each other, replace what you imagine about each other with a little something about who you really are." He closes his eyes for a minute, as though trying to find the wisdom of Solomon. "Hand me your questions. I'll cross off question number seven and give you another question at the bottom of the list, but not because somebody threw a tantrum."

When he hands us back his list, I read the new question: *What is one thing you like about me?* That question is worse than *When have you ever felt scared?* Thanks a lot, Gwen Turner!

The end-of-the-day bell rings, and thankfully there's no time for any more interview questions.

As we're gathering our satchels, Mr. Duncan says, "Here's a note for your parents. For your homework, take some time to think about your interview questions. And no running down the hallway!" And though I don't run down the hallway, I run all the way home, glad to be out of the principal's office, and away from Gwen.

When I hear Mama get home that evening, I start practicing my duet louder than I had been practicing, and wait for her to come up. When she does, she sits next to me on my bed. I lay my flute down on my lap. She lays Mr. Duncan's letter still in its sealed envelope on hers.

"How did your day go?" Mama asks.

"Fine," I say, though it went about as fine as skipping in too-small shoes.

"When I read Mr. Duncan's letter," she asks, "will it confirm that it went fine?"

Not being sure what Mr. Duncan wrote, I decide to lay everything on the table. "I got all my schoolwork done. I kept playing the duet with Gwen, even though it sounded awful. I didn't poke Gwen even though she poked me. And I asked Gwen Mr. Duncan's questions, even though I didn't want to, and Gwen didn't want to answer them. That's fine-ish, right?"

"Well...," Mama says, thinking on it. "It's a fine start."

Mama takes out Mr. Duncan's letter and silently reads it. He must not have mentioned anything beyond what I confessed, because Mama's face doesn't stitch an inch of being upset.

"While I make supper," Mama says, returning Mr. Duncan's letter to its envelope, "you keep practicing your duet." She stands to leave. "I'm proud of you, by the way, for selling out of your chicken and dumplings. Miss Greta told me that

Mr. Johnson came by to share the good news and has asked you to make more. Congratulations!"

"Thank you, Mama!" I say, glad to have a reason to smile. "Then it's okay with you if we make more?"

"It's okay," she says.

Later that evening, with chicken and dumplings back on my mind, I remember the jar I "fixed" for Mr. Coles. I wonder if he ate it. If he did eat it, will he tell everyone everywhere that they should not buy jars of my mama's chicken and dumplings from Mr. Johnson's store because it tastes awful? If Mr. Coles does tell everyone, will Mr. Johnson have wasted his hard-earned money purchasing supplies for Miss Greta and me to can more? Maybe Mr. Coles noticed that the seal on the jar was popped and didn't eat the contents. After all, everyone knows that when the seal on a jar is broken what's inside is likely bad.

I decide to write Mr. Coles an apology just in case he tried the jar with the hot-spicy additions I put inside. I'm sure Caesar will deliver the note to Mr. Coles tomorrow if I ask him to do it for me. And so I begin.

> Dear Mr. Coles,
> If you haven't already, please do NOT eat the chicken and dumplings I gave you, just throw the jar away. I added something I shouldn't have. I'm also sorry about what happened with Gwen. I'm doing my best to take her off my NOT-friend list, but it's very, VERY hard.

Sincerely,
Your first-chair flautist,
Allie

P.S. If you want to take my mama dancing again, I'll try to understand, but I'm thinking it's Gwen you should be worried about, not me.

twenty-five
GETTING MITZY BACK

In the morning, Mr. Duncan asks Gwen and me to sit back down in the chairs in front of his desk, and pick up where we left off with our interviews.

As Gwen is answering *What is your favorite memory?* I can't help but smile. Imagining Mr. Coles dressed up as a clown makes me laugh, too. When she answers question number nine—*What do you love about your family and your community?* I can't help but think that's what I love, too—everyone looks out for us kids in the neighborhood so no matter where you go, you feel safe. And when she answers the question *What qualities do you feel make for a good friend?* I can't help but think we are on the same page, because knowing someone will always stick by you, even when you're down, is what I loved about Jewel.

But when I get to the last question that Mr. Duncan added to the bottom of the list—*What is one thing you like about me?*—Gwen just sits and sits without answering. Is it really *that* hard for her to answer?

Mr. Duncan must notice the silence, because he leans forward and says, "I have found that I am a whole lot happier if I focus on the good in my life, in myself, and in others.

It's sort of like what prospectors out West do when panning for gold. They might have a bucket full of rocks, but it's that gold nugget they run home and tell their families about."

I don't think Gwen is paying attention to Mr. Duncan's analogy, because when he asks her the thing-you-like-about-Allie question again, Gwen's lips are rubber-cemented.

"Miss Turner?" Mr. Duncan says. "I'm waiting."

"I like... I like... I like the way she sings at church."

"When have you heard me sing?" I say, thinking Gwen just made up something to get Mr. Duncan's eyes off her. "I've never had a solo."

She squints at me. "I've heard you belting plenty of times, whenever you're sitting near our family."

"Enough of that," Mr. Duncan says.

After I write down what Gwen said about my singing voice, Mr. Duncan tells Gwen to begin her interview of me, and so she does.

As I'm answering questions one through five, I make my answers as short as possible.

Why do I like playing the flute?

"Because I play it well."

What is my favorite subject in school and why?

"Band, because I play the flute well."

What is my favorite season and why?

"Fall, because we have our fall concert."

What would I like to do when I grow up?

"Play at Carnegie Hall."

What do I do well outside of school? I would say play my

flute, but because I don't own one, I can't really say I do it well outside of school, so I say drawing maps instead.

Seeing Gwen write down my answers to those first questions warm my thoughts, like I warm my flute when I'm blowing hot air into the mouthpiece. So when Gwen asks me "What is your favorite memory?" and I don't see an I'm-better-than-you smirk on her face, I decide to give her another for-real answer.

"My favorite memory is when Jewel and I were at the park. We were imagining we were wearing long, flowing gowns from France and had on white gloves and glistening shoes. We were riding inside a horse-drawn carriage, which was carrying us up the mountain to attend a ball at Monticello. We imagined that when we went inside, we danced with the kindest gentlemen until the Great Clock's gong sounded. And when it did, we got to choose which gentleman we'd marry. Of course I chose the one who lived in a faraway kingdom where only what is right and fair happened, and nothing fine or good ever got broken."

All at once, as if holding my breath beneath water, I wait for Gwen to say something that will make me wish I hadn't just shared with her one of my favorite memories. But Gwen doesn't make fun. She's just writing on her paper like she doesn't want to forget the details.

When she's done writing, Gwen looks at me and says, "You miss Jewel a lot, don't you?"

"I do!" I say.

"Does she like living in Chicago?"

Though Gwen didn't laugh at my memory, I'm not about to tell her I don't know what's going on with Jewel since Jewel hasn't replied to my letters yet. So all I tell Gwen is, "I hope Jewel hasn't gotten polio."

Gwen's eyes get big. "I hope not! I worry about getting polio."

"Me too," I say.

"Mary, my best friend, moved to Ohio this summer."

"I'm sorry," I say, wondering why I hadn't noticed Mary wasn't in our class on the first day of school. I guess I should have noticed, especially when Gwen grabbed Mitzy. Mary probably would've been right there if she hadn't moved to Ohio, and then I'd be stuck writing two biographical sketches for Mr. Duncan, one about Gwen and one about Mary.

After a few minutes of quiet, Gwen finishes asking me the rest of Mr. Duncan's interview questions. And for some reason, I really don't know why, by the time she asks me the question that replaced number seven, *What is the one thing you like about me?*, the answer comes out easily.

"I like how you hold your daddy's hand when you're leaving a concert. I like how you have three sisters, live in a big house, and have everything a girl could ever want. I like how smart you are, how well you play the flute..." I stop myself, realizing I've given Gwen way more than one thing I like about her.

Gwen laughs then.

"What's so funny?" I say, wondering if she's laughing at me.

"It's funny," she says, "I like some of the same things about you! I like how you hold your mama's hand when you're leaving a concert. I like how smart you are and how well you play the flute. There's only one big difference—I sometimes wish I was an only child like you, because I have to share my mother with my sisters, but you get to have your mama all to yourself, which I think would be perfect."

And though I'm hearing Gwen's words, I'm really not believing it! She thinks MY life is perfect? How strange is that?

"Please push your desks and chairs back," Mr. Duncan says, and he's wide-smiling. "Time for you young ladies to turn your interviews into sketches. After that, get started on your schoolwork."

When I get home, I look up at Mitzy still on top of the icebox. I know better than to ask for her. Though Miss Greta washed Mitzy's face, ironed her dress, and got her dressed yesterday, her hair is still a mess. I quick-look away from my doll. I grab the saucer of cookies and the glass of milk Miss Greta has put out for my snack, and sit down at the table to eat. Miss Greta comes into the kitchen then.

"Thanks for the snack, Miss Greta," I say with a mouth full of cookies.

"You're welcome," Miss Greta says. "But gracious me, don't eat so fast!"

"I won't," I say, but my cookies are already gone.

"Did you behave yourself in the principal's office today?"

"Of course I did." Then I echo her advice. "I wouldn't want to act a fool and grieve my mama."

Miss Greta smiles. "You think you're cute, don't you?"

"Very!" I say.

"Let's get started on those chicken and dumplings for Mr. Johnson."

And Miss Greta and I set our hands to work on canning twenty-four more jars of chicken and dumplings.

That evening after Mama comes into my room with Mr. Duncan's letter about today, I see she's already opened it, so I decide to tell her about the interviews, the biographical sketches, how Gwen wrote something nice about me, and how I wrote something nice about her.

I ask her, "Did he put my biographical sketch of Gwen in the envelope? Did I get a good grade?"

"You did! Forty out of forty! That is excellent, Allie." Mama takes the sketch out of the envelope and hands it to me. "Will you read it to me?"

"Of course!" I say, and so I do.

"That is very well written!" Mama says when I get to the end. "Good enough for your school's newspaper!" which makes me wonder if Mr. Duncan will recommend me for the staff of the *Jeffersonian* when I get into sixth grade.

On Thursday, Gwen and I do our assignments. We eat lunch together. We practice our duet together. While playing, we try to look at each other and smile. Mostly, I try to remember the good things Gwen said about me, and the good things I said about her.

Finally, it's Friday, my last day of being stuck in Mr. Duncan's office.

As I'm working, I notice something interesting. I can hear Gwen's pages turning at about the exact same time I hear mine turning. I can hear her pencil scratching against the paper at about the exact same time I hear mine scratching. I can hear her yawning at about the exact same time I hear myself yawning. And for some reason, the echo of Gwen working in the principal's office at the same time I'm working makes me feel less alone during this last day of being in trouble.

During lunch, I decide to ask Gwen a question that Mr. Duncan didn't think of.

"Hey Gwen, what's the best joke you've ever heard Caesar tell?"

"Oh," she says, smiling. "I like the one 'What do you call a snow woman?'"

And at the exact time, we're saying, "A snow ma'am!"

"Caesar is the best!" Gwen says.

"I know," I say. "He is."

When it's time to practice our duet, Gwen and I stand right next to each other. We begin each measure at the exact same time. It isn't perfect, but it's not too shabby either.

When the end-of-the-day bell rings, Mr. Duncan tells Gwen and me to have a nice weekend and that we can return to Mrs. McGinness's class on Monday. "Don't give me a reason to have you in here again," he adds.

"No, sir," we say at the same time.

Gwen and I walk down the hall together. It's not like we're friends or anything. She will never, ever replace Jewel. No one will. But some kind of weight has been lifted between Gwen and me. It's almost like my inside heat toward her has been left out in the cold and turned into a snow ma'am.

Caesar and Booker T. are standing outside of Mrs. McGinness's classroom. I think they're waiting for us.

"Hello, my ladies!" Caesar says like he's some colonial gentleman. "Did you miss being in class with me?"

"Of course I missed you!" I say. "It wasn't fun being stuck in the principal's office all week."

"Just making sure," Caesar says.

Booker T. says, "Class, band, lunch, especially recess has been sooooo boring without you two clowns."

"Who are you calling clowns?" Gwen says, and she soft punches his arm.

"Ow!" he says, though I doubt it hurt.

"Instead of you two playing a duet during the concert," says Booker T., "maybe we should put you together in a boxing ring and sell tickets."

"That's not funny!" Gwen and I say at the same time.

"Speaking of the concert," Caesar says as we head out of the building and down the steps, "I'm playing a snare drum solo!"

"Nice!" Gwen and I say at the same time.

"Oh!" Caesar says to me, "I almost forgot. These are for you."

"Thanks," I say.

Caesar hands me two envelopes, one from Mrs. McGinness and one from Mr. Coles. I put them in my satchel to read later.

"See you clowns Monday," Caesar says. Then he gets into Uncle John's truck with Jocelyn to head home.

After we wave goodbye to Caesar, Booker T. turns toward

Gwen and me, and deepens his voice. "May I walk you both home?"

Gwen shakes her head. "My dad said I have to walk with Evelyn, my annoying sister, this week on account of being in trouble."

"Maybe another time," Booker T. says.

"Maybe," Gwen says, and she walks toward the high school to meet her older sister, who's about Jocelyn's age.

"How about you?" Booker T. asks me with his still-pretending-to-be older voice.

"Sure," I say. "But don't get any fool ideas."

Booker T. looks at me like he has no clue what a fool idea is, which is fine by me.

When I get home, I smell oatmeal-and-raisin cookies Miss Greta has made for me. I don't mind looking at Mitzy today while I'm eating my snack, because I am 99.9 percent sure that when Mama reads Mr. Duncan's letter later, I'll be getting her back. When I get to telling Miss Greta about how Gwen and I like the same joke Caesar tells, I notice the strangest thing. Her eyes are on the brink of tears. "I knew you could do it!" she says. Then she gives my forehead a big kiss. What's gotten into Miss Greta?

After my snack, I go upstairs to read what's inside the envelopes Mrs. McGinness and Mr. Coles have addressed to me. Mrs. McGinness has put my *Aesop's Fables* homework in her envelope. In red ink across the top, she's written: *What an interesting lesson you got from the story. And I love your drawing! Well done! I look forward to having you back in class.*

While I'm opening my envelope from Mr. Coles, my heart starts *thump-thump-thumping* I'm hoping he won't be mad about those extra spices.

> *Dear Miss Lewis,*
>
> *I am looking forward to hearing you and Gwen play your duet. I heard from Miss Perkins that you've been working hard. Remember, practice makes perfect.*
>
> *With regards to your chicken and dumplings, I have been meaning to tell you, thank you! I ate the entire contents the day after your mother gave it to me. It was quite delicious! I loved the spicy kick! Mr. Johnson is on the money by selling them at his store! Keep up the entrepreneurial spirit. Save your profits, and in a few years, you'll have enough to buy your very own flute.*

I hadn't thought of that! Maybe by next year I can buy my own flute with my share of the profits. And if I add that "kick" to Mama's recipe, maybe Mr. Johnson will sell even more jars!

I finish reading Mr. Coles's letter.

> *Yours truly,*
> *Mr. Coles*
>
> *P.S. Tell your mother Mr. Coles's dancing shoes are ready to roll!*

And though I like Mr. Coles's letter, I'm not 100 percent sure I like the P.S. part, but later that evening I decide to let Mama read my letter, even though it's addressed just to me.

"What's this about a spicy kick?" Mama asks me after reading Mr. Coles's letter.

"Oh, I just added a little extra spice, that's all."

Mama smiles then. "I've got an idea. Let's invite Mr. Coles, Mr. Johnson, and Gwen over for a meal, then afterward you and Gwen can practice your duet for us, and I can talk to Mr. Johnson about how your chicken-and-dumplings enterprise is going. What do you think about that?"

"You want to invite Mr. Johnson *and* Mr. Coles at the same time?"

"Why not?"

And though I can think of a hundred reasons why Mama should not invite both misters to come over at the same time, instead of arguing with her, I decide to change the subject.

"Mama, can I please have Mitzy back now?"

"Yes, ma'am! Let's go get her."

Suppertime feels almost perfect that evening. I don't have to look at Mitzy on the icebox. I don't have to worry about sitting in the principal's office come Monday. And I don't have any inside heat when thinking about Mama going dancing with Mr. Coles. Still, a lump of sadness creeps into my thoughts when I think about Jewel.

"Mama, why hasn't Jewel written to me?"

"I don't know, Allie. It takes time to get settled into a new home and city, and not everyone likes to write as much as you do."

"I'd be happy with just a drawing," I say.

"I'm sure you'll hear from her soon."

"I hope she and Mr. Poindexter are okay."

"Me too," says Mama.

twenty-six
LESS BROKEN THAN YESTERDAY

That Sunday after church, Mama makes a beeline for Mr. Coles, who is sitting with Gwen's family. I know she's inviting him and Gwen over for supper the following Friday. I know she's telling them it'll be just a pot of beans with country ham and some corn bread, something light before Gwen and I practice our duet. I can see Mr. Coles hard-nodding yes, and Gwen shrugging a guess-so yes. Next, Mama finds Mr. Johnson in the crowd to invite him. I see him saying yes, too.

The following school week goes by fast, and the Friday evening Mama planned for Gwen and me to practice our duet arrives. Despite the red heart I kept on my map above the antiques store, Mama and Mr. Johnson are all-business the entire night.

Despite the black heart I had drawn on my map above the school but couldn't erase, Mama and Mr. Coles are everything but band-business the entire night.

Despite everything I have ever felt about Gwen Turner, we manage to get through that evening without any spills, without anything mean being said, and without either of us messing up too badly on our duet.

Even though I'm still positive that Mr. Johnson is the better mister for Mama, and I'm certain I'd rather not be related to Gwen, I don't butt into Mama's business. I had promised myself and her that I would mind my own, which meant putting my Man-for-Mama Plan into my drawer and forgetting about it.

And so all night, I focus on talking with Mr. Johnson about the interesting things he has in his antiques store, and about how to run a good business selling chicken and dumplings. And I concentrate on getting Mr. Coles's opinion on how my flute-playing can be improved.

And not once that entire evening did my inside heat rise. It was like minding my own business kept it frozen.

Finally, it's the night of our Fall School Band Concert. I can barely sit still while Mama hot-combs my hair straight and shiny like a new penny, but I try my best. I don't want my ears to get burned. As soon as she's done, I run upstairs and finish getting ready.

My shoes are already polished. My Sunday dress is already pressed and laid out on my bed. And my flute is already inside its case, sparkling clean. I'm ready to play my duet with Gwen. We've practiced together so many times we probably can play it without the music.

"You look nice, Mama," I say when it's time to leave.

"Why, thank you," she says, and places her pocketbook in the crook of her arm. "You don't look too shabby yourself."

We head out the door and begin walking toward the

auditorium inside the newer Jefferson School, the one with the junior and high school grades that sits behind my school that only goes up through fifth grade.

"It's a lovely evening," Mama says, and she squeezes my hand gently. "Look at the halo around the moon. I suspect it'll rain later."

I look up and see the moon shining like a giant spotlight inside a circle above the streets of Charlottesville. The sky's night clouds are dancing in dark blue gowns inside the moon's soft glow. I take a deep breath and enjoy the smell of the fallen leaves that are crunching beneath my feet.

"Mama?" I say. "Mr. Johnson is still coming to see me play tonight, right?"

"Yes, he is," Mama says.

"He makes a good friend for you, doesn't he?"

"Yes, he does."

"It would be a shame for someone as nice as Mr. Johnson to stay a confirmed bachelor. Don't you agree? Miss Greta, of course, is way too old for Mr. Johnson. But what about Iris? Miss Greta's niece?"

Mama laughs like I'm kidding around.

"I'm being serious, Mama. Mr. Johnson needs to get married. He'll make some little girl a perfect daddy."

But Mama doesn't agree or disagree with me. All she says is, "What am I going to do with you, Alexandra Lewis?"

Inside the high school's band room, Caesar comes running up to me. "Hey Allie Cat! Are you and Gwen ready for your duet?"

"Of course," I say. "Are you ready for your solo?"

♥ 174 ♥

"You know it... *man!*"

"I'm no man," I say, though I know full well Caesar is just trying to sound like he plays in a jazz band.

Just then, Gwen, wearing a yellow dress and yellow ribbon in her hair, and Booker T., wearing a black bow tie and slicked-back hair, join us.

"You look *FANnnn TASss TICK!*" Booker T. says to me, which for some strange reason makes my cheeks get warm.

"You look like as fine as Cab Calloway!" I reply, which for some strange reason makes Booker T.'s cheeks turn red and Caesar and Gwen laugh.

But before my inside heat can rise at Gwen and Caesar for laughing at me, Mr. Coles is tapping the conductor stand and telling us all to take our seats and get out our instruments, so we can tune.

From her second chair, Gwen leans over and asks me, "Are you nervous?"

"A little," I say.

"But we've practiced," she says. "We'll do okay, right?"

"We'll do great," I say, though deep down, I'm kind of worried I'll be the one messing up, first chair or not, especially if I look out and see the audience.

Once we've tuned, Mr. Coles says, "All right, band, I know that tonight you'll play your best. You'll play your best because you've all practiced. You'll play your best because you want to do your school proud. You'll play your best because you are the best. Are you ready to put on a concert to make Jefferson School proud?"

"Ready!" we all say.

Then we stand with our instruments and music in hand, leave the band room, and head out to the auditorium where Mr. Coles has already set up rows of chairs, music stands, and the drums on the stage.

The flutes and clarinets file into the first row. The saxophones and trumpets file into the second. The trombone and tuba players file in at the back with all the percussion players. Once we're in front of our stands, we wait for Mr. Coles to walk up to his conductor podium and motion with his hands for us to be seated. When he does, we sit down. And for the very first time, I'm in first chair at the front of a room overflowing with just about every colored family of Charlottesville. I quick-look away from the crowd.

Mr. Coles *tat-tat-tats* his stand with his baton, and as one, we lift our instruments, ready to play. The audience instantly becomes quiet, and our concert begins.

First, we play Beethoven's sonata, then Mozart's minuet. Next, we play a waltz, then a polka. Afterward, we play a song that sounds like we're at the circus, all the while Booker T.'s mallets are flying. The audience hoots when we're done. Next comes my favorite piece, a jazz number composed by Count Basie. During that piece, Caesar goes wild on the snare drum! The audience hoots and hollers when his going-wild solo is done and I want to hoot and holler, too, but I have to keep playing my flute.

After Count Basie's song, Mr. Coles bows, then proudpoints back at us. The audience claps so long it gets me worried about our duet being the last number on the program. But that's how Mr. Coles lined it up. Our duet is the final piece of the night.

Mr. Coles nods at us. Gwen and I stand up with our flutes. I walk to the front of the stage with Gwen. We place our music on our stands that are so close to each other that my flute almost touches Gwen's shoulder. As Mr. Coles gets seated at the piano, I do not look at the audience, only at the music. And when I hear Mr. Coles begin playing the prelude, Gwen and I raise our flutes to our lips. Then I take a deep breath and we begin.

From my flute, notes come skipping like raindrops on Fourth Street. From Gwen's flute, notes come slipping like rainwater cruising down West Main Street. From both our flutes, notes come swirling, twirling, trilling, and spilling like a rain ballet above all the streets of Vinegar Hill.

When Gwen and I finish playing, a hand-clapping roar begins, and for the first time it's not just for Gwen, but for Gwen *and* me. I look out at the audience. Everyone is standing, proud-smiling and clapping. Mama is standing, proud-smiling and clapping. Jocelyn, with Junebug *buzawuzzawuzzing* on her hip, is standing, proud-smiling and clapping. Aunt Lavern and Uncle John are standing, proud-smiling and clapping. Mr. Johnson, Miss Greta, Chops... everyone is giving us a standing ovation.

I hear Caesar from behind me saying, "That's my cousin! She sure can play!"

Gwen and I look at each other and we can't help but proud-smile, too. And then we curtsy like real ladies do.

Back in the band room, Booker T. comes over and says to Gwen and me, "You guys were amazing!"

I say, "We're *girls*, not guys!"

"Whatever," he says, rolling his eyes.

Mr. Coles comes over. "Well done, Miss Lewis and Miss Turner! You played most excellently! And, as they say, well-played music is the stuff that makes life sweet."

"Thank you, Uncle Raymond," Gwen says, hugging him.

"Thank you, Mr. Coles," I say, though I'm not about to hug him like he's my daddy.

Caesar comes over. He puts one arm around me and one around Gwen. "Hey, Mr. Coles," he says, "I've been thinking. When you marry Aunt Elizabeth, Allie, Gwen, and me will be same-age cousins! We can call ourselves 'The Triplets' like we're a jazz band. How about that!"

And just like that Mr. Coles's light brown cheeks turn bright red, so I bop Caesar on the arm.

"*OW!*" he says, being all dramatic.

"You'll be okay," Gwen says.

Once I've put my flute back in my case, Caesar and I leave the band room, and go out to the auditorium to find our family in the crowd. They're standing together with Mr. Johnson and Miss Greta.

"Thanks for coming," I say to Mr. Johnson.

"I wouldn't have missed it for the world," he says. "By the way... I have something for you." And what does Mr. Johnson hold up while spreading the widest smile a human being can smile? A flute case.

"Thanks," I say. "But I really don't need a flute case."

"It's not just a case," he says. "Open it!"

When I open the case, I can't quite believe what I'm seeing! It's a flute, sparkling like dew on grass at dawn! "You bought me a new flute? A brand-new flute? And it's all mine?"

"It's all yours! But it's not new," he says. "Someone brought it into my shop on consignment a few days ago, and of course I thought of you. Your mama paid down most of the cost. Miss Greta and I agreed to use our share of the profits from the chicken and dumplings toward it, and your uncle John made up the difference. How about that!"

"It's... it's absolutely PERFECT!!!!!" I say, and I tackle Mr. Johnson with a hug, practically knocking him over. I tackle Miss Greta with a hug, practically knocking her over. I tackle Uncle John with a hug, practically knocking him over. Then I hug Mama, and keep hugging her, too, because nothing about this moment in time is broken.

When I'm done hugging Mama, I can't help but spin and dance and whirl, because this here girl is holding her very own flute!

"Watch it!" Jocelyn says as I'm whirling. "You're about to step on my shoes, and I just polished them!"

When I'm done not stepping on Jocelyn's shoes, I hear Caesar asking Mr. Johnson, "Do you think any of your customers will be bringing in a drum set? Having my own drums would be out of this world!"

"In my house?" Aunt Lavern says. "I don't think so!" which makes everyone but Caesar laugh.

While we're laughing, Gwen comes up to Caesar and me. "My parents want to know if all of you would like to come over for some coffee and chocolate cake. Mr. Johnson and Miss Greta, you're welcome, too."

"Really?" I say, not quite believing what I'm hearing. "You're inviting us to your house?"

"Actually...my uncle is the one doing the inviting, and he says you won't regret it because no one makes chocolate cake like my mama."

"I don't know about that," I say, and I feel my head shaking a little. "Because I'm pretty sure my mama makes the best chocolate cake in all of Charlottesville!"

"We'll see about that," Gwen says, her head shaking the same as mine.

"Enough of that," Mama says. "We probably use the same recipe."

When we go outside to walk toward Gwen's house, it's raining, but it's okay, all the grown-ups have brought umbrellas. Mr. Coles's umbrella is big enough for himself, Mama, and me. Uncle John's is big enough for Aunt Lavern, Chops, and Junebug. Mr. Turner's is big enough for Mrs. Turner and Gwen's two little sisters. Mr. Johnson's is big enough for him and Caesar. Miss Greta's is big enough for herself. And Jocelyn has one big enough for her, Gwen's older sister Evelyn, and Gwen.

While we're walking, the sound of the rain hitting Mr. Coles's umbrella is low and sweet like a quiet hymn. I tight-squeeze my very own flute in my left hand, and tight-squeeze Mama's left hand with my right. Mama's right hand is holding on to the crook of Mr. Coles's arm that's holding on to the umbrella. Above the rain, I hear Caesar, who is holding my used-to-be flute, making a proposal to Mr. Johnson. He wants to make wooden toys to sell at his store. Above the pitter-patter, I hear Jocelyn telling Evelyn about the importance of applying Noxzema before going to bed to keep one's complexion spotless. Despite the drops falling, I hear the one sound of all of our footsteps *smat-smat-smatting* on Commerce Street as we walk toward Gwen's house.

Pretty soon, the rain stops, and all of us are at Gwen's house, and I'm walking up the grand steps of the Turners' place and going inside! Once inside, we take off our shoes, and Gwen's mama hangs up our coats. The ladies—Mrs. Turner, Mama, Miss Greta, Aunt Lavern, Jocelyn, and Evelyn head to the kitchen to get the coffee percolating and to slice and serve the chocolate cake, while the gentlemen and boys find a seat in the living room. While everyone is getting situated, I look over Gwen Turner's house and quickly realize three things: the house looks bigger on the outside than it does on the inside, the furniture is not as grand or fancy as I supposed it would be, and when Gwen's daddy sits in his chair, he doesn't smile one bit. He just sits there, blowing out puffs on a smelly pipe, and sort of frowns. Who knew his face could look so grumpy?

"Hey, Allie," Gwen says. "Follow me. I want to show you something."

But something about the way Gwen says *Follow me* makes me worried, so I say, "I'm telling you right now, Gwen Turner, if you play some fool joke on me, I'm saying something to Caesar."

"No jokes tonight but Caesar's. I promise," she says, so I follow her into her room, the one she obviously shares with Evelyn.

Gwen pulls out a box from her closet and opens the lid.

"Look," she says, holding up a doll. "This is mine. My grandfather gave it to me when I was a baby."

"She's just like Mitzy!" I say.

"I know. The exact same doll. I guess they were bought around the same time!"

"She is beautiful," I say.

It's true. Gwen's doll is beautiful. Her dress is the brightest blue. Her hair looks like it's never been mussed. Her pink cheeks have not faded one bit. It looks like Gwen's doll hasn't spent one hour outside of its box. And though Gwen's doll looks brand-new, I'm thinking her doll is not half as beautiful as my Mitzy.

Caesar comes poking his head into Gwen's room, and with his mouth full says, "Come on! This chocolate cake is the best!" And so Gwen and I hurry ourselves downstairs to eat our share of cake that cannot possibly be as good as Mama's.

That evening, after my pajamas are on and I'm in bed with Mitzy close, I lean my head on the softness Mama's body makes.

"Thank you again, Mama," I say, "for pitching in with Miss Greta, Uncle John, and Mr. Johnson to buy me my very own flute. I'm truly grateful."

Mama smiles. "Thank you for playing that beautiful duet. Thank you for being kind to Gwen. And thank you for not stomping your feet through mud puddles all the way home just because Mr. Coles and I were holding hands tonight."

"Oh...," I say, "I guess I forgot to get mad."

Mama and I laugh then.

"You know what, Mama?"

"What?"

"This evening turned out pretty amazing, even though it turned out nothing at all like I would have planned it."

"It was amazing. Speaking of plans...tomorrow, Raymond—Mr. Coles—will be taking us to the mountains in Gwen's daddy's car for a picnic! How about you bring your flute and play for us? Doesn't that sound like a perfect Saturday?"

"There's no such thing as perfect, Mama. Remember?"

"Don't go sassing me, child." But I know from her tone that Mama knows I'm only teasing her.

"Will you make fried chicken and potato salad for the picnic? I love your potato salad!"

"I might," Mama says while tucking me in. "It's time for you to say your prayers." And so I do, an out-loud one.

"Thank you, Lord, for all that I have—for my mama, my brand-new flute, for Mr. Johnson being like an uncle, my not-perfect doll, my cousin Caesar, and most of all, for getting Gwen off my NOT-friend list. It wasn't easy, but having her off that list makes me feel better somehow. And thank you for the potato salad I'll be having tomorrow."

"Amen," Mama says after me. "Amen!"

Mama gets up and leans over to kiss me good night.

Just as she is about to leave, she reaches into her dress pocket. "I almost forgot. This came in the mail for you today. I was saving the best for last."

It's a letter from Jewel!

"Shall I keep the light on so you can read it?"

"Yes, please," I say.

And even though I've already said my prayers, I rip the envelope open, and start reading!

> Dear Allie,
> I'm sorry it took me so long to write! You wouldn't believe how busy I've been with helping my grandfather get settled, and meeting my cousins, and starting school. I never knew I had so many relatives!
> Chicago is much bigger than Charlottesville. You would love 47th Street! There's a theater, much bigger than the Paramount, and we don't have to sit in the balcony unless we want to! Oh, you would LOVE the shops on 47th Street! They are way fancier than the ones on East Main Street!
> My school is so big I got lost the first day. Don't worry, I eventually found my way. And there are several fifth-grade classrooms, not just one like at Jefferson School. My grandfather is doing well, and no one in my family has gotten polio. I don't have my own room. I have to sleep with my great-aunt who not only snores worse than Miss Greta, she steals the covers!
> I wish you could play with me in my school band and march with me during the Bud Billiken Parade. I'd love to see you wearing one of our uniforms with HUGE, furry hats! Only thing, there is NO WAY you'd get first chair in this band. Sorry to say, but it is true. These city girls and boys can really PLAY!

Don't worry. You'll always be my BEST friend, even though we live hundreds of miles apart. I hope Mr. Johnson sells tons of your mama's chicken and dumplings, and that you get a daddy SOON.

Find enclosed a picture I've drawn for you. Next time you write, tell me what you think of it.

Love,
Jewel

P.S. Tell Caesar and Booker T. I said hi.

I look over Gwen's beautiful drawing. She and I are lying down on the grass in front of our oak tree at Washington Park. We're looking up at two clouds, daydreaming. Inside the cloud above my head, she's drawn a man and woman getting married. Inside the cloud above her head, she's drawn a lady doctor listening to an old man's heart. Obviously, the lady doctor is Jewel and the old man is Mr. Poindexter. I love Jewel's picture!

I decide not to wait until morning to draw something for Jewel.

I fling off my covers, skip over to my dresser, take out a piece of paper and my tin of crayons, and draw the picnic I'll be having tomorrow. I draw the mountains blue. I draw the blanket purple. I draw the plates with brown fried chicken and yellow potato salad. I draw my flute gray. I draw Mama and me light brown. But when I draw Mr. Coles I disguise him. He's lying down on the blanket with his hat covering his face like he's shading it from the noonday sun. Above the blanket, I draw a fluffy cloud with a perfect red heart above it. Below the cloud I write *Guess who?*

No sooner do I finish my drawing, which is as perfect as a chicken-and-dumpling Sunday, than a great big sneaky smile spreads across my face, because I'm thinking Jewel will never figure out the mister.

AUTHOR'S NOTE

Do you find inspiration when you discover histories of communities pulling together, of people persevering for the sake of the children, of men and women prevailing despite winds of injustice? I do! That's why I set *Mama's Chicken and Dumplings* in 1930s Vinegar Hill, in the midst of the Jim Crow era.

Despite Jim Crow laws enforcing segregation and casting heavy shadows upon every corner of African American life, and overt racism running rampant, especially in the South during those years, Vinegar Hill was a thriving African American business and residential community, albeit a small one, within the city limits of Charlottesville, Virginia. Similar communities rose from the darkness throughout the nation.

When doing research for this novel, I quickly realized that volumes of nonfiction could be written about Vinegar Hill. Volume 1 could include the many successful African American entrepreneurs who lived and/or worked there. Folks like: George Pinkney Inge, who opened his grocery in 1891; Nannie Cox Jackson, a Jefferson School educator who owned a great deal of real estate in Charlottesville, and whose family operated a successful billboard advertising company; and Thomas J. Sellers, who founded two local newspapers for African American readers. Vinegar Hill's West Main Street would also hold a prominent place in that volume. All kinds of shops—owned and operated by persevering African

Americans, some who had once been enslaved—offered goods and services to residents of color who were refused entry elsewhere. Some African American business owners of Charlottesville gained enough wealth to own fine homes not only in Vinegar Hill, but also in the Starr Hill neighborhood that was right next door.

A 1930s view of the 200-block of West Main Street, home to many African-American businesses.

Vinegar Hill's volume 2 could easily be filled with the history behind Jefferson School, which was founded as a freedmen's school for African Americans not long after the Civil War ended. Jefferson School educated all the African American youth living in and around Charlottesville, including the children of Vinegar Hill. In 1926, Jefferson School's high school was completed and generations of its graduates attended historically Black colleges and obtained degrees in the fields of medicine, science, engineering, mathematics, and more.

A volume about Jefferson School would surely include the numerous educators and administrators who inspired the school's students—folks like: Isabella Gibbons, who taught herself to read while enslaved and who was one of the school's first teachers; principals Owen Duncan, Booker T. Reaves, Cora B. Duke, and Benjamin E. Tonsler, who served at his post for thirty years; and well-loved Rebecca Fuller McGinness, who taught the younger grades at Jefferson School for decades and lived to be 107.

Vinegar Hill's volume 3 would likely focus on the community's social, political, and religious activities: the women's literary clubs and aid societies like the Daughters of Zion Mutual Aid Society that sought dignified burial places for those in the African American community; the men's fraternal clubs like the Elks, Masons, and Shriners; the Boy Scouts, and the high school students' dramatic club, debate team, marching band, choir, science club, and football team. The Daughters of Zion Hall, which was the community's gathering place to discuss important issues, would also be included.

Washington Park, the city's only public park open to African Americans in the 1930s, would surely hold a place in this Vinegar Hill volume, as would the park's red barn where local African American singing groups like Sampson's Happy Pals performed. Washington Park was located on land deeded to the City of Charlottesville in 1926 by Paul Goodloe McIntire, who had donated two parcels of land—one for a park for African Americans (9.2 acres) and one for European Americans (92 acres). In 2001, Washington Park was renamed Booker T. Washington Park. Volume 3 would be remiss if it did not include the rich history behind the places of worship attended by Vinegar Hill residents, like First Baptist Church (then on West Main Street) and Zion Union Baptist Church (then on Fourth Street NW).

Volume 4 about Vinegar Hill could easily be filled with the life stories of the tireless African Americans who offered necessary professional services to Charlottesville residents, especially since other establishments closed their doors to those of African descent. Histories of George Rutherford Ferguson, Sr., George R. Johnson, and Edward W. Stratton, physicians; John Andrew Jackson, a dentist; and John Ferris Bell, a funeral home director and undertaker, to name a few.

As an African American, it's my hope that *Mama's Chicken and Dumplings* pays tribute to the people and places that made Vinegar Hill an amazing, thriving community. To honor the residents of Vinegar Hill, I used family names I found in my research—Lewis, Coles, Johnson, Turner, and Poindexter, to name a few. I also used the last names of more prominent citizens in the community and had them working within their occupations, though they may not have done so in the year my story takes place.

Though I did a ton of research to get the details right in *Mama's Chicken and Dumplings*, for the sake of story, I did take some liberties. I placed the character named Gwen in a handsome home on Commerce Street. More likely, her family would have owned a home in the Starr Hill neighborhood. But then, Allie would not have crossed paths with Gwen on the way to school. I have the character Caesar attending Jefferson School, though he lives in Albemarle County. More likely, he would have attended Albemarle Training School. But then, Allie and her cousin would not have been in school together.

Unfortunately, you can no longer walk most of the city blocks that once formed the Vinegar Hill neighborhood. The City of Charlottesville deemed it a slum and razed the community in the 1960s in the name of urban renewal and development. Still, you can catch a glimpse of its former glory by viewing archival photos of the people and the places that made up the historic neighborhood. You can tour the building that once was Jefferson's high school at the Jefferson School African American Heritage Center in Charlottesville. And if you put a penny in your pocket and skip down to the corner of Fourth Street NW and West Main, you'll be able to easily imagine being ten years old, on your way to Inge's Grocery, where the original building still stands, to buy yourself a Mary Jane.

Resources to Peek Back Into Time

(A complete bibliography for this book as well as a recipe for making Southern style chicken and dumplings may be found on the author's website: https://www.dionnalmann.com/mamas-chicken--dumplings.html.)

Audio Files and Film Clips

The Amazing Interplanetary Adventures of Flash Gordon, 1935 audio files. https://archive.org/details/Flash_Gordon1935, accessed July 9, 2023.

"Rare 1920s Footage: All-Black Towns Living the American Dream." *National Geographic*, https://www.youtube.com/watch?v=1_dKmtCWWao, accessed July 27, 2023.

Books

Douglas, Andrea, ed. *Pride Overcomes Prejudice: A History of Charlottesville's African American School.* Charlottesville, VA: Jefferson School African American Heritage Center, 2013.

Lewis, Edna. *The Taste of Country Cooking.* New York: Alfred A. Knopf, 1976; reissued 2006.

Osvalds, Gundars, Scot French, and Kenneth Schwartz. *Vinegar Hill 1963: Life in the Neighborhood.* Charlottesville,

VA: Jefferson School African American Heritage Center, 2015–2020.

Documentaries

In the Fullness of Time. Produced by Elizabeth Howard Productions, narrated by Rita Dove. Virginia Humanities Digital Archive: 2004. https://www.discoveryvirginia.org/islandora/object/islandora%3A11072, accessed December 25, 2022.

Raised/Razed. Produced by Jody Yager and Lorenzo Dickerson, edited by Randall Taylor. Maupintown Media: 2022. https://vpm.org/raisedrazed, accessed December 24, 2022.

That World Is Gone: Race and Displacement in a Southern Town. Produced by Scot French, directed by Hannah Ayers and Lance Warren. Field Studio Films: July 1, 2012. https://www.fieldstudiofilms.com/that-world-is-gone/, accessed December 25, 2022.

West Main Street. Produced by Chris Farina and Reid Oechslin. Rosalia Films: 1995. https://vimeo.com/273521741, accessed April 27, 2023.

Images

Rufus Holsinger's African American Images. *RWHolsingerphotos.org.* https://rwholsingerphotos.org/images.php, accessed April 7, 2023.

Websites

Holsinger Studio Portrait Project. A showcase for the *Visions of Progress: Portraits of Dignity, Style, and Racial Uplift* exhibition held at the University of Virginia's Albert and Shirley Small Special Collections Library in Charlottesville from September 22, 2022 through June 24, 2023, https://holsinger.iath.virginia.edu/, accessed August 20, 2023.

Picture Me As I Am. An interactive story map hosted by the Jefferson School African American Heritage Center in Charlottesville. https://storymaps.arcgis.com/stories/096ae9182d3a4667a06fb428f962c69e, accessed May 7, 2023.

ACKNOWLEDGMENTS

I would like to acknowledge the amazing special collections librarians at the University of Virginia for their help with my research; my SCBWI friends of the pen—Ellen B., Kathy E., Moira D., and Tamara T.—for cheering me on as I forged my way along this crazy writing endeavor; my agents, Kelly Dyksterhouse and Jacqui Lipton, for taking me on; my husband for paying the bills so I could write; and most importantly my editor-extraordinaire, Margaret Ferguson, for seeing promise in my manuscript and showing me how to give it wings.